Cleopatra's New Attitude

Sometimes the grass is greener on the other side

Mercedes M. Alexander

AuthorHouse™
1663 Liberty Drive
Bloomington, IN 47403
www.authorhouse.com
Phone: 1-800-839-8640

© *2012 by Mercedes M. Alexander. All rights reserved.*

No part of this book may be reproduced, stored in a retrieval system, or transmitted by any means without the written permission of the author.

Published by AuthorHouse   03/07/2012

ISBN: 978-1-4685-6163-0 (sc)
ISBN: 978-1-4685-6162-3 (hc)
ISBN: 978-1-4685-6164-7 (e)

Library of Congress Control Number: 2012904363

Any people depicted in stock imagery provided by Thinkstock are models, and such images are being used for illustrative purposes only.
Certain stock imagery © Thinkstock.

This book is printed on acid-free paper.

Because of the dynamic nature of the Internet, any web addresses or links contained in this book may have changed since publication and may no longer be valid. The views expressed in this work are solely those of the author and do not necessarily reflect the views of the publisher, and the publisher hereby disclaims any responsibility for them.

PROLOGUE

"Forbidden Fruit Creates A Strange Jam." *Well ain't that the truth*, thought Cleopatra Beavers as she passed the sign on the local church marquee. It had been three weeks since she had decided to cool her friendship with Leonard 'Mr. Thought He Was Slick' Wilkins, and she was starting to think how close she had come to compromising herself over the last year. Leonard was the man she thought was her friend and was fast becoming more than that, but was not her husband and proved to be one of the biggest liars she had ever met. He had talked his way into her life by wooing her with his love poems, promises and constant attention and was later exposed as a womanizer the entire time he was chasing after her. She had been warned and her friends tried to help her plow her way through the relationship by telling her step by step what she needed to do to put the dog in his place. Cleo could not believe she had been caught up in such a web of deceit, but here she was licking her wounds with one huge consolation, she was proud of the fact that she was woman enough to turn her back on him and walk away while her self-respect was still intact. She had learned through her experience with Leonard that the grass is not always greener on the other side and a leopard never changes his spots.

Mercedes M. Alexander

Moving on with her life was top priority for Cleo. But fate had other plans and things beyond her control would put her back in the path of the one man she had promised herself to stay away from—Leonard Wilkins.

CHAPTER 1

"Forbidden Fruit"

It all started so innocently. Cleopatra Beavers and her husband, Michael, frequented almost every charity event in the city having any type of involvement with children. Cleo was an avid supporter of children's charities and Michael just tagged along because he had no choice. This particular evening was one of elegance and sponsored by the Governor and his wife. Everybody who was anybody was there and food and drinks were in abundance. Cleopatra was unaware of eyes following her around the room and did not know that she had been spotted and would be the target of interest for one of the most recognized and important guest of the evening.

Leonard Wilkins was watching Cleo as she and her husband went through the receiving line during the reception. Leonard was one of the city's most eligible bachelors, and was also a big supporter of this particular charity. He had a soft spot in his heart when it came to children and did whatever he could to support organizations geared to helping them. He was given award after award for his charitable contributions and was recognized by people as one of the city's top players in the social and political arena. Leonard

Mercedes M. Alexander

was having a good time and was on the prowl that night. Looking around the room, Leonard spotted a beautiful female who looked as if she could easily be any man's dream woman. He watched Cleo as she casually strutted through the line making her way to where he stood. Her movements and the smile she wore took his breath away, he was totally mesmerized. Leonard was immediately impressed by the woman and could not understand the feeling he had washing over his entire being while observing her. "Who is that woman in the silver dress showing every curve in her body?" Leonard asked his associate, Ray Stiller, standing next to him.

"Oh that's Cleopatra Beavers," replied Ray. "Man, don't get any ideas about her, she is not your type and won't give you the time of day. Besides, she's married to that large man following close behind her like a watch dog. Don't think he won't go up side your head if he thinks you have an inkling of an idea about flirting with her."

Leonard eyed the man following behind Cleopatra and decided instantly that he was not up on his game as a husband by letting his wife float through the crowd dressed in such a seductive dress and smiling that dazzling smile at every man in the place. If she were his wife, he would have her on his arm and every man at the event would know who she belonged to and that she was untouchable. Nope, this woman was just ripe for his plucking and pluck he would if he got the chance. Just like the dog he was and the fact that he was told she would not give him the time of day, Leonard was immediately stricken with the thought of proving Ray to be wrong. He quickly turned his charms on as soon as she approached him.

"My, what a lovely dress on such a lovely woman! It must have been tailor-made just for you and I don't believe any other woman in this city could wear it and look as great in it as you do."

Cleopatra's New Attitude

Cleo looked up into the face of someone she had seen before but could not put a finger on just where. *He must be joking*, she thought, *that line is old and lame.* Cocking her head to the side she quickly determined by looking at the man that he was harmless. "Thank you very much; I don't believe I caught your name."

Leonard grabbed her hand and lightly kissed it as he bowed. "Leonard Wilkins and I am at your service anytime my fair lady. Here's my card just in case you need anything."

Oh my God, he's really piling on the bull crap and I'll probably need waders to get out of this one. "I'm sure I won't need your services, however it was very nice of you to make such a grand offer." With that, Cleo snatched her hand away, gave his card back to him, and sashayed right past him trying to restrain herself from laughing aloud.

Standing in the receiving line and a little stunned at the woman's quick dismissal of him, Leonard was very embarrassed by her flippant attitude. "Did you hear that little twit," Leonard sneered toward Ray. "She snubbed me in front of my colleagues and switched her little behind right on down the line."

Ray looked at him in astonishment. "Don't you think you put it on a little strong? It was obvious what you had on your mind the second you laid eyes on her. She would have had to be blind, crippled and crazy not to see you coming with your smooth line of pimp talk. I applaud the woman for cutting you short."

Leonard, not to be outdone, moved through the crowd very slowly so that he could see Cleopatra as she greeted people she knew. He noticed her taking her husband's arm and holding on tightly when she got a glimpse of him watching her. *He's one lucky man*, thought Leonard, *but a woman like that needs special attention and he just does not look as if he knows how to supply that attention. I could easily make her the star in my parade and she would be the perfect trophy for a man of my status.*

Cleopatra was enjoying herself and even though she had to drag her husband along, she was sure he was having a good time. Cleo is the type of person who likes to socialize, mingle with a lot of people, and always comfortable talking with anyone. This affair had proven to be one of the best she had ever attended. The music was good, the food was terrific, and the most important people in the city were in attendance. She knew she was being watched as she moved about the room and had an eerie feeling that this man would cross her path again.

After the affair, Leonard Wilkins was walking back to his Jag with one thing on his mind; *I need to show little Miss Beavers that I don't take kindly to being dismissed and that I always get what I want.* After getting into his car and revving up the engine he sped out of the parking garage and in his mind started his plotting to get as close to Cleopatra as possible. He would find out her habits, where she worked, what she liked, who she hung out with and most of all her weaknesses.

Cleo, as she and her husband Michael headed for home, thought nothing of her encounter with the silly man. She had her mind on what she needed to do the next day at work. If only she knew what the next few weeks would bring, maybe she could have saved herself a lot of pain and sorrow in the future.

CHAPTER 2

"What you see is not always, what you get . . . ."

Cleopatra Beavers was a workaholic and enjoyed her job as a sales associate for the Marriott Hotel in downtown Memphis. She had been working in the hospitality industry for close to twenty years and found that every day brought on a new challenge and interesting people into her life. She had a knack for making friends. Her clients and associates were very comfortable with the knowledge that she would always get the job done and do it well. Her life was one of church, family, home and friends. She pretty much put all of her priorities in that order and never neglected any of them. Now in her forties, she had settled into a lifestyle that was not extravagant but one of ease and comfort.

Her marriage to Michael Beavers was one of necessity. Cleo, always being the "good girl", was a senior in college and still a virgin until the star football player at Memphis State University started dating her. Michael never really pressured her for sex but strongly suggested it every time they went out on a date. His pleas of how much he loved her and if she loved him she would give it up kept her upset. Her friends in the dormitory were

Mercedes M. Alexander

always bragging about their boyfriends and how much they enjoyed sex. According to them, it was the next best thing to sliced bread and once you started you couldn't stop. She listened time and time again about what the other girls did and how they were able to get a man to do whatever they wanted if they gave them a little "coochie." Some of her friends were even sleeping with their professors and getting A's in classes they never bothered to attend. A few of them were sleeping with men they met off campus and getting them to buy clothes and jewelry for them. Cleopatra thought this was on the same level as prostitution and knew that she could never do such things. Not wanting the other girls to know that she was still a virgin, she just kept her mouth shut and laugh at their exploits. They all thought she was sleeping with Michael because he only had eyes for her and the fact that she never spoke about it and only smiled at their tales confirmed their suspicions that she was indeed having sex with him. Not being up on sex and just what she needed to do to protect herself and afraid to ask any of the other girls about birth control, Cleo ended up pregnant just weeks after she gave her "cookies" to Michael. Although the sex was not good to her, she kept giving it up with the hope that it would get better. It never got better, but something was put in the oven and the little loaf of bread was rising and well on its way before she realized she was pregnant. When she told Michael of her suspicions, he started grinning from ear to ear. He had loved Cleo from their first date and now she was having his child. His first and only thought was to marry her and start a life he knew would be a happy one. Cleo, on the other hand, was scared out of her wits and cried herself to sleep for days. Once the pregnancy was confirmed, she and Michael approached her parents with the news.

The quickie wedding was not what Cleo had always dreamed she would plan, but her parents insisted that it take place immediately and little time was given for planning. Her mother was a socialite in the Black community and her father was the pastor of Bethel Baptist Church, one of the biggest Black churches in the city. Cleo's parents only concern was what Pastor Handy's congregation and their friends would think about Cleopatra being pregnant and not married. The good Reverend Byron Handy could not stand in his pulpit and preach to his congregation about the sins of the flesh with his daughter carrying a bastard child. No, this situation would be rectified in the only way possible, marriage. The usual fussing over a bride-to-be was denied to Cleo and her wants were not considered. She was pregnant and she would be married and soon. Her mother took the reins and planned within four weeks the wedding of a lifetime. It was a beautiful affair with the best of everything. Mrs. Handy had spent a ton of money putting on the dog for her friends. Cleopatra was her only child and this was the only time Della Handy would be able to have the wedding she never had. She would live out her dream of a big wedding through Cleo and everything would be exactly as Della Handy had dreamed. Before she knew it, Cleopatra was married, had graduated from college, was sticking out like a watermelon and waiting for the arrival of her baby in the sweltering heat of a Memphis summer.

Michael landed a job on the high school level as a football coach for the upcoming school year and found them a nice little apartment close to his job. Being the star quarterback at Memphis State gave his some kudos when he decided to apply for the position at local high school. His dreams of playing pro football were dashed when he tore his knee to pieces during the last game of his senior year at Memphis State. Although he was devastated by the injury, he was content with the knowledge that he had Cleopatra to have and to hold for the rest of his life and he had a child on the way to make their lives complete. In his mind, all was right with the world and he had it by a string.

On July 3rd, Cleo's water broke and the pains started coming immediately afterwards. As Michael was speeding to the hospital, Cleo started thinking about her little bundle of joy and how much she would shower the child with love. She knew her life was about to make a drastic change and was anticipating holding her baby in her arms. While she was being prepped for delivery, Michael made phone calls to both their parents. When Michael returned to the delivery room, he was told the baby was coming fast and this would not be a long labor for Cleo. He quickly put on the scrubs handed to him and eagerly rubbed his hands together in anticipation of the birth of his child.

The pains were starting to come very close and were more intense than Cleo had expected. Then the pains became excruciating and Cleo could not help but scream, as they seemed to rip her body in half. Her training to help with the pains from Lamaze classes was useless and she immediately sensed that something was wrong. She saw the doctor and nurses running in and out of the room and a look of concern on Michael's face. Her last recollection was that of a mask being put on her face and someone saying "this doesn't look good . . . ."

*   *   *

"Mrs. Beavers" a soft voice was saying to her as she slowly opened her eyes. Cleo did not know how long she had been knocked out. She blinked her eyes a few times to focus and tried to ask what had happened. "Is it a girl or a boy?" she asked through her daze.

Her mother leaned close to her and kissed her on the forehead while Michael stood there with a look of shock on his face. Reverend Handy stood with tears running down his cheeks and prayed aloud.

"I'm sorry Mrs. Beavers," the Doctor said as the nurse was scribbling on her chart. "We could not save your baby."

The last thing Cleo heard was her own screaming. She woke up a day later to begin a life without her child. Cleopatra Handy Beavers was soon to learn that she would never again bare a child because of complications with the delivery and the performance of a lifesaving hysterectomy. Her life was now altered in the most meaningful way. She had no baby, no chance of ever having one and now she had doubts about loving Michael.

*   *   *

Leonard Wilkins was a 45-year-old wannabe cat daddy and was well known throughout Memphis as one of the most powerful contractors in the city. His company did very well and there were examples of his accomplishments all around the Memphis city skyline. He was also known for his fooling around with the ladies and his weakness for the younger ones. He may not have been the most handsome man on the block, but his money and power made him look good to a lot of women. They fed his ego constantly and he never failed to buy whomever and whatever he wanted. Money was no object and according to him, any female could be bought.

Leonard LeAndrew Wilkins was born to a single mother in the projects of Memphis, Tennessee. He never knew his father and at the age of five

Mercedes M. Alexander

was sent to his grandparents by his mother because she decided she was too young to be tied down with a child. He would never see his mother again as she got caught up with the wrong crowd and died from a drug overdose at twenty-six years of age. His grandparents were attentive to Leonard's needs and made sure their only grandchild paid close attention to his grades in school. Leonard proved to be a brilliant student and received a full paid scholarship to Payne College in Tennessee, and acquired his graduate degree in engineering at North Carolina A&T University.

While attending North Carolina A&T University, Leonard hooked up with a group of aspiring students and became a member of the Phi Beta Sigma Fraternity. Since this fraternity was the most popular on campus, the girls were always hanging around and willing to do whatever it took to get a Sigma man who would probably turn out to be a good provider as a husband. Leonard quickly learned how much in demand he was and made the decision to spread his love around to as many girls as he possibly could. His playa way of life became natural to him and he began to take all women for granted.

His marriage to a college sweetheart did not last long once she came to the realization that Leonard enjoyed the ladies and cheating was always going to be a part of his profile. Melissa Wilkins had come to know early in the marriage that Leonard always kept one of his whores working in his office and never tried to hide the fact that she would spread her legs whenever and wherever he pleased. She had a few jealous and bitchy friends who took glee in telling her what they saw and heard about Leonard and his fooling around. Hearing all of this was embarrassing and to top it all off she accidentally walked in on him in his office with one of his women. Melissa packed her bags, did like the cowboys, and "got the hell out of Dodge" before Michael knew anything and she never looked back.

It proved to be very dangerous to many young females in the city now that Leonard was divorced and on the prowl. He always claimed to be a lover, not a fighter, and used his wits to waylay boyfriends and husbands of the women he messed around with. Scruples were not a part of Leonard's mental make-up. The man dangled three and four women at a time, wooing them and making each one of them feel they were the love of his life. His explanation to his male friends who knew about the many different women was that he needed all of them because each one served a different purpose. Most of his married male friends knew that one day Leonard would meet his "Waterloo" and they all wanted to be around to meet the woman who would make him her lap dog.

Flying by the seat of his pants and screwing around with whomever he could get to drop her panties became second nature to him, and he played the game well. He was prosperous and happy with his lifestyle until one Cleopatra Beavers walked into his life. He would now have to pull out all the stops and concentrate, as he never had before to get past the brick wall she had built around her. There was something about Cleo that made him experience feelings he never had toward any woman. His first thought was that she looked good to him and he wanted to make her one of his conquest to talk about in his later years in life. His second thought was that she was the type of woman who would never be anything other than number one with any man. He never knew just what love was and he would eventually come to the realization there was someone beyond his reach that did not give a damn about who he was. When love did strike Leonard, it was almost too late.

Chapter 3

"If this world were mine . . . ."

"Cleo, there's a large bouquet of roses at the front desk with your name on it honey", exclaimed Paul Nyugen, who thought he was the only gay Vietnamese man in Memphis, Tennessee and better known as Poopie. Being so tiny, wearing make-up and his long black hair in a ponytail deceived most people into thinking they were dealing with a woman when they first met him. However, when he opened his mouth, there was no doubt he was a man perpetrating a fraud. He spent most of his time switching around and sticking his nose in matters that did not concern him. This morning, instead of being in the back office at his desk checking the daily schedule, he was at the front desk watching the flowers being signed for by the receptionist and hoping they were for him. Poopie's lover had walked out on him during the weekend and moved in with someone else. The little man was heartbroken but just knew that his "friend" would come to his senses and return. To his disgust, the flowers were for Cleopatra and it sent him into a tizzy wanting to know who had sent them.

When Cleo went to retrieve the flowers she was surprised to find there was not a card attached to the bouquet. They were her favorite roses—yellow with a hint of red around the edges. She had no idea as to who would send three dozen roses to her. If it had been six roses or even a dozen she would have immediately thought of Michael, but knowing him, he would not spring for such an extravagant surprise. Michael may have been her husband and loved her dearly but he was not one to hand out surprises, especially when they cost as much as three dozen roses.

"Ok girlfriend, just who are those gorgeous flowers from and what did you do so special to deserve them?" Poopie questioned while snatching the empty envelope from her hand. "Girl, you must have put out the booty to get this, someone spent money on these babies. Is there a mystery man in your life thanking your for a good time?"

"Poopie, get out of my business and take your narrow butt back to your desk. Whoever sent them just forgot to put the card in the envelope. I'm sure I'll get a call today from the sender to ask if I like them. Just go back to your little closet and stay out of my business."

"For your information sistah, I've been out of my "little closet" for a long time," chuckled Poopie. "Well, when you find out who sent the flowers please let me know. Whoever that man is can check me out because he's the type that could have my heart." With that, Poopie snapped his fingers and walked seductively back to his desk.

Cleo only laughed at the little queen and took the flowers back to her desk.

*   *   *

Monday's flower delivery was Cleo's first big surprise. For four weeks in a row on Monday morning, a large bouquet of yellow roses was delivered to her without a name on them. She never mentioned it to Michael or any of her friends because she did not have an inkling of an idea as to who was sending them or why.

Week five approached and a gold box with red ribbon was delivered to Cleo. In the box were exquisite gold hoop earrings. Week six brought a beautifully carved heart shaped gold necklace with a nice size diamond in the middle of the heart. Week seven presented her with a real Gucci purse and matching key chain and week eight was a gift certificate for a whole day of pampering to one of the most expensive day spas in town.

With each arriving gift, the office gossip grew. Of course, the main cheerleader and grapevine informer was Poopie. He was beside himself trying to get Cleo to tell him who the mystery man was, and Cleo telling him that she did not know just added fuel to the fire. The other women in the office were starting to talk behind Cleo's back. They were dead sure she was lying and knew exactly who was sending the gifts. If truth were to be told, the gossip was being spread by a group of jealous women wishing somebody thought enough of them to send one yellow rose.

This has got to stop, thought Cleo, *I have to find out who this mystery person is and why they are showering me with gifts.* She called the florist and found that the flowers were paid with cash and the sender insisted no card be sent. They could only tell her that it was a well-dressed Black man driving a black jaguar. The jewelry store could give her no leads and the people at the day spa said they did not know who purchased her gift certificate but were told that she was to have the best and her anonymous benefactor had left a one hundred dollar tip to make sure she was pampered.

Bewildered and not knowing what to do sent Cleo running to her best friend, Patricia Jackson. Pat laughed at her concerns at first and told her to

Mercedes M. Alexander

enjoy her blessings. However, she thought about it again and told her to be careful and more watchful of her surroundings because she could easily be the target of a stalker.

"Pat, just who would be stalking me?" "I'm not the type to think I'm somebody special, and I can't think of anyone who would do such a thing. Besides, I don't think a stalker would be sending such extravagant gifts."

"Well you just don't know, there are a lot of sick people out there and the rich people seem to be the sickest nowadays. Just promise me you will be careful and if it keeps up much longer, you need to tell Michael. Hell, I know he's going to hit the roof when he finds out how long you've been receiving these gifts and didn't bother to tell him, but it may get to the point where you need to be safe rather than sorry."

Pat's last comment sent a shiver through Cleo. She knew that she should have told Michael about the first gift, but she never thought it would go this far. He would not only hit the roof, he would make it his business to find her admirer and probably punch his lights out. Although Michael seemed to be mild mannered and quiet, he had a temper that exploded at a very high level when it came to Cleo and her happiness. He was also a jealous man and the thought of some man sending her anything would push him over the edge. Cleo decided then and there she had let this go on too long and telling Michael now would only make matters worse. This had to be something she would deal with alone and she had to be discrete about it.

Giving her friend a hug as she was leaving, Cleopatra gave her the gift certificate to the spa and told her to go and get pampered since she had no intention of using it.

Cleopatra's New Attitude

* * *

Week nine came around and no gift! Cleo had gotten into the habit of looking forward to seeing what the new week would bring her. To her dismay, the week passed and nothing arrived for her. She thought maybe her admirer had grown tired and decided to drop her from his weekly shopping sprees. While walking into her favorite spot for lunch on that Friday, something happened and everything fell in place.

Cleo had a habit of eating her lunch every Friday at an Italian restaurant a few blocks from her job. She sat at the same table almost every week and ordered the same chicken parmesan dish. On this particular Friday, she casually strolled to the restaurant enjoying the fresh air. Cleopatra entered the restaurant at her usual time and immediately looked for Ramone, her friend and the best waiter in the place. As she stood waiting to be seated, she noticed a nicely dressed man sitting at the table Ramone always held for her on Fridays staring directly at her.

The waiter walked her way, "Hello Ms. Cleo, it's good to see you as usual. There is someone waiting at your table who said he was your lunch date for today. I hope you don't mind that I went ahead and had him seated."

"Ramone, I don't have a lunch date today and I don't think I know that man".

As Cleo squinted her eyes to get a better look at the man, it suddenly hit her who he was. It was the asshole from the charity reception who thought he was all that and a bag of chips. Before she could open her mouth, he had sprinted from the table and was standing at her side.

"Thank you Ramone, I'll take it from here", Leonard spoke with much authority. "Well, well, Ms. Cleopatra Beavers, we meet again. This time I hope we can hit it off and at least be friends."

"Sorry, Mr. whatever your name is, I don't think I made any plans to have lunch with you and quite frankly I prefer to eat alone."

"Oh but you must have lunch with me, I brought the wallet to match your Gucci purse and I know you will love it".

Cleopatra was caught off guard as she stood with her mouth opened. Leonard quickly seized the moment and guided her to the table. Now all of the pieces were starting to fall into place. This man was the bearer of the gifts and now was weaseling his way into her lunch hour. Whatever his motive was, Cleo was sure she would not like it and braced herself for a showdown.

CHAPTER 4

"Fools rush in . . . ."

Cleo stood and refused to sit when Leonard ushered her to the table. She was standing with her arms folded and legs slightly apart. Anybody looking in his or her direction would immediately know there was trouble brewing by her stance.

"Alright buddy, just who the hell are you and what are you up to?" sneered Cleo as she jerked her arm from his grasp leaving Leonard with a startled look on his face. He had never had a woman to confront him and look at him as though he were some kind of snake that had just crawled from under a rock. He quickly gathered his composure and nervously put his hands to his side to show that he meant no harm in touching her.

"Look Cleopatra, I know we got off to a bad start, but I would just like to get to know you. I thought the little surprises would tweak your interest and make you think that someone thought you were a very special woman needing to be pampered. I was not sure how to approach you so I decided to try something different. Don't you remember me from the Children's Charity event? I'm Leonard Wilkins the one you ignored in the receiving line after making your remarks to make me look and feel small. I

Mercedes M. Alexander

know we got off to a bad start that night and I take responsibility for that, I just wanted to rectify the situation and get to know you."

Cleo immediately started to chuckle, she had heard horror stories about Mr. Leonard Wilkins and could not believe he was standing here in the flesh confessing that he had been wooing her the last eight weeks in an incognito fashion. "Well Mr. Wilkins, I must say that never in my wildest dreams would I have imagined you stooping so low to impress a woman. What's the matter—losing your touch and having to resort to buying women nowadays?"

Leonard could feel a boil coming from his stomach and slowly rising toward his head. He knew this woman would not be compromised, and he just may have blown his chance of really getting to know her. "Ok, I apologize for my tactics and promise not to pull anything like this again. Just have lunch with me and maybe we can be friends, I see that you are not the type to be blown over by me or probably any man." He stood with the look of a wounded animal on his face and dropped his eyes to the ground. "If you decide after lunch not to talk to me again, I will never contact you in the future. Agreed?"

"I think that's fair enough and I want you to know upfront that I don't intend to ever see you again after today."

Cleo took her seat as Leonard, trying to be the perfect gentleman, ran around to push her seat gently under the table. As she took her napkin to place it in her lap she noticed that his hands were slightly shaking when he lifted his napkin from the table and wondered if she had really upset him to the point that she had made him nervous.

"Look, Mr. Wilkins . . ."

"Please call me Leonard, Mr. Wilkins was my grandfather."

Cleopatra's New Attitude

"Alright Leonard, I'm sorry if I exploded and seemed rude but you must understand that I'm a married woman, I don't appreciate strange men sending me gifts and I don't like my space being invaded. I don't mess around and you're wasting your time if you think otherwise."

"I guess I need to apologize to you also. Please believe me when I say that I have never done this before but when I thought of you, I immediately saw a woman who deserved to be pampered and one that I wanted to get to know. If you say that we can only be friends, I will accept that. However, I must warn you that I do take my friends out to lunch on occasion and sometimes I send gifts on their birthdays."

Cleopatra couldn't help but chuckle, the puppy dog look on the man's face was hilarious. "You never give up, do you? Let's just have lunch and leave the friendship thing up for grabs for now—agreed?"

"Whatever you say Cleo, I just wanted to meet you and get to know you," replied Leonard with his mind still working overtime, scheming as to what he needed to do next to get this woman exactly where he wanted her—in bed.

CHAPTER 5

"What's come over me . . . ."

Their lunch turned out to be a pleasant one. Leonard put on his best behavior and proved to be witty and intelligent. He made light jokes about his business and told Cleo his entire life story. She was impressed that someone who came from such humble beginnings had made such a success of himself. She also noticed how nicely he dressed and that his hands were professionally manicured. Cleo was always one to notice a man's hands. She thought if a man took the time to take care of his hands, he also took care of the rest of his body and from the looks of how that tailored-made suit caressed his well built body, she knew he was the total package.

"Since I monopolized the entire lunch talking about myself Cleopatra, we must do this again so that I can give you equal time."

"Equal time is not necessary Leonard, my life is not as colorful as yours and my accomplishments could not compare to all you have achieved."

"Oh, but it is necessary. I would love to hear about your work with your sorority, the Junior League, your church and even your job at the Marriott."

Cleo looked at him not believing what she had just heard. He obviously had been inquiring about her because she had not told him anything and yet he knew about things he had to snoop around to find out.

"Yes you have done some homework because you seem to know things about me already. Tell me, do you always snoop around to find out things about your friends?"

"As a matter of fact, I don't. I just couldn't help myself and when I found how well loved you are by your family and friends, I knew you were something special. I know a lot of women who could not count a number of good friends on one hand and you seem to be able to collect them at will."

"I learned at an early age Leonard that you have to be a good friend to have a good friend. Friendship is something you cannot take lightly. If my girlfriend is hurting, I hurt. If she is needs something, I want to be there it help her with it. I know women who can only say they have one friend and that one friend usually hangs around because they pity the woman or wants something from her. To me, that's a testament of a woman who is pitiful and is to be pitied."

Leonard leaned back in his chair and smiled. He was beginning to like Cleo more than he really wanted to and her presence was once again giving him a feeling of something he could not explain. He just sat in his chair staring at Cleopatra and wondering just what it would be like having her around all the time. Talking to her was so easy and she proved to be an attentive listener who could give him the exact feedback he needed. Leonard was wearing a huge smile on his face and had a feeling of contentment. Little did he know that the warm feeling growing within him was something that could prove to be dangerous to his player way of life.

Cleopatra's New Attitude

"Well, I have to get going and thanks for the lunch." Cleo quickly rose and stuck her hand out for a friendly handshake and thank-you.

Leonard took her hand in his and a shiver ran up his spine. *Just what is this woman doing to me*, he thought as he bent to kiss her hand. "Please have lunch with me next week, same time, same place. I will not cross the line and promise to be a very good boy." He put the Gucci wallet in her hands and nodded his farewell with a slight twinkle in his eyes.

His smile was contagious and Cleo quickly accepted and hurried out of the restaurant. She could feel his eyes on her backside as she walked away and they felt as if they bore right into her in places they had no business being.

Arriving at her office, Cleo forgot she had the Gucci wallet in her hand and walked into the office running into the one person she did not want to see, Ms. Poopie. Of all people to run into, she had to run into the only person who could look at that wallet and start putting two and two together. She hastily tried to stuff the wallet in her purse but was not fast enough. The little queen had already spotted the wallet and was fast approaching her.

"Girl just where have you been and is that Gucci wallet the real thing?"

Before she could answer, Poopie had snatched the wallet from her hands and was examining it thoroughly. He had an eye for name brand items and this was one of the times his expertise in spotting the real thing did not fail him. "Well I'll be damn, this thing is real and what is this tucked in the side."

Cleo tried to grab the wallet but Poopie was too quick for her and pulled the little note card out and began reading it aloud.

"To a woman who could steal any man's heart and one I would like to know better. L.W. Ok, now I know you've been giving up the booty and just who is L.W."

Laughing at the little jackass, Cleo finally got her chance and snatched the wallet. She calmly walked away leaving Poopie tapping his foot and waiting for an answer, one that he would never get from her.

*　*　*

The very next week as Cleopatra approached her Friday lunch spot, there stood Leonard outside the door with one yellow rose in his hand. She smiled as she quickly realized that she was actually happy to see him and looked forward to another lunch with him doing all the talking and entertaining her.

"Well hello, funny meeting you here", Leonard exclaimed as she came closer. He immediately let his eyes scan the entire length of her body, from her hair lightly swinging around her shoulders to the cute little red sling back heels on her tiny feet. "I'm here only if you allow me to stay. I did promise not to be pushy and I still want to be your friend."

"Come along, since you're here there's no need in sending you away. If you promise to entertain me and keep the conversation light, I promise to be nice."

Leonard was thrilled with her response and throughout the lunch kept her in stitches describing his shenanigans as a child. His playfulness and quick wit made him a great person to hold a conversation with and Cleo wondered if he was always this way with people. She was secretly loving the attention and deep down inside knew that she was playing with fire.

Cleopatra's New Attitude

It was not her intention to lead Leonard on and make him think she wanted anything more to do with him than just a friendship. However, her presence only gave him the impression that he had a chance to get closer to her and he was loving every minute of it.

"Leonard, I don't want you to get the wrong idea about me letting you invade my lunch hour for the second time. I have a lot of male friends, but they don't pursue me and send extravagant gifts. I know where I stand with them and there is a line they never cross. I'm not too sure you are willing to accept the boundaries I will set for you in order for us to be "just friends". I'm also uneasy being seen with you because of your reputation with the ladies. I don't need any jealous woman getting in my face about you. That's a lot of drama I can do without."

Leonard raised his eyebrows and chuckled. "Does that mean you have thought about me crossing that line?

"No it does not, it only means we need to reach an understanding, and you need to stop buying flowers and other gifts. My friendship does not come with a price, but my heart does and that is a price I know you cannot afford. Besides, I don't need a man, I have one at home and I am perfectly content with him.

"Well Cleopatra Beavers, being content with a man and being in love with him are two different things. I think I detected a hint of contentment out of necessity without the attachment of love."

Cleo was stunned. The man was too inquisitive and hit a raw nerve. Love was something that faded from her life a long time ago and she had no room for it now. She had closed that door and went through the motions of life efficiently and without emotions.

"Listen Leonard Wilkins, if you want to keep my friendship there are two subjects that are taboo, one being my love life and the other being my husband. My friends don't snoop in my business and if they do, they don't remain as friends for long."

Leonard threw his hands up in the air as if to defend himself from Cleo's biting words. He knew this was a battle he could afford to lose in order to win the war in the weeks and months to come.

"Ok little lady, have it as you wish, we can just be friends and I promise to stay in my place and stay out of your personal business."

As they finished their lunch, Cleo was apprehensive about Leonard's intentions. The way he looked at her at times was something that made her self-conscious. He had a way of looking at her as if she were the only person in a room or as if she was something he longed to have. He was attentive to her needs as no man had ever been and she was beginning to experience some guilt by having lunch with him. She was also starting to enjoy the attention and knew Leonard's possible intent could eventually become dangerous.

Leonard was at his best proving to be a delightful lunch buddy and making the hour pass swiftly. However, Leonard was still laying his trap and would prove to be a fox in the hen house if Cleo ever let down her guard.

CHAPTER 6

"Betcha by golly wow . . . ."

Weeks turned into months and every Friday Leonard and Cleo had lunch together. Spring, summer and fall had quickly passed and their friendship had gotten to the point where they occasionally called one another during the week just to chat. Their chatting was always on the light side. They talked about politics, their families, friends and work. She had become quite comfortable with him and looked forward to the Friday lunches and the friendly bantering.

During the Christmas holidays they agreed to exchange gifts and met on their usual Friday lunch date. However, Cleopatra had told Leonard they should have a cost limit of $50 for gifts to each other. She went out and found him the perfect gift—a pair of black driving gloves with the Jaguar emblem raised on the leather. Leonard, being the person he was, went out and purchased a pair of stunning two carrot emerald shaped diamond earrings. He presented them to her during one of their Friday lunch dates. When Cleopatra told him she could not accept the gift, he lied and told her they were CZ's that his friend at the jewelry store said were the best fakes you could buy. She then decided she could accept them and thanked him for such a beautiful gift. He immediately insisted that she put them on so he could see how they looked hanging from her ears. Cleo was hesitant about putting them on and Leonard teasingly told her not to worry about her ears rotting off because although the stones were be fake, the gold was real. Cleo put them on for her friend's satisfaction and looked at them in her ears with her compact mirror. They were indeed beautiful!

Sitting in a corner of the restaurant and hidden between booths was Poopie. He had long found out that Cleopatra was meeting someone during her Friday lunches but had not found out exactly who the man was. Following her today was the third time he had seen her with Leonard, and Poopie was determined to learn the name of the mystery man. From the glistening of those earrings in Cleo's ears, he was sure they were real!

*   *   *

On the first Friday of the New Year, Cleo turned the radio on in her car to listen to the news on her way to work. The storyline for the morning was about a large fire in downtown Memphis that had completely destroyed a large section of a local shopping area. As she listened closely, she quickly realized the area they mentioned housed Luggi's Italian Restaurant and she immediately thought of Leonard.

What if he doesn't hear the news and goes to the restaurant looking for me? Cleo became quite concern about Leonard not knowing about their favorite spot and decided to call him at his office as soon as she got settled at work. She normally called him on his cell phone because that was the only number she had. When he didn't answer his cell she looked up his office number in the phone book and called.

Cleopatra's New Attitude

"May I speak to Mr. Leonard Wilkins please?" Cleo crisply said into the phone to a receptionist who sounded no more than sixteen years old and was smacking gum into the phone as she talked.

"Sure, can "ya" hold on a minute', came the woman's reply after popping her gum in Cleo's ear for the third time.

As Cleo held the phone waiting for Leonard to pick-up she wondered how he could have someone so unprofessional answering the phone at his place of business. Didn't he know that first impressions are lasting ones, even on the phone people form opinions about how a business is run and word of mouth could kill any business. She made a mental note to tell him about the lack of business savvy the young woman had by chewing her gum in the phone and her unprofessional use of the English language. In the middle of her thoughts, Leonard came on the line with a voice smooth as silk and humming in her ear in a deep baritone timbre.

"Hello, Leonard Wilkins, may I be of service to you"

"Hi Leonard, it's Cleopatra. I didn't know if you heard the news about Luggi's burning this morning and I didn't want you going over there to meet me for lunch today thinking the place was still there."

What's this, thought Leonard with a big smile on his face. *The little lady is now calling me out of what?—concern?* "Thank you for calling Cleo, I did not hear about the fire. Just what do you propose we do now that our favorite eating place is gone?"

"I don't know Leonard, maybe we should just forget about lunch today. I'm not sure if this isn't an omen that we need to give our little Friday lunch meeting a rest for a while.

Panic immediately rose in Leonard's mind, she was not going to slip away from him this easily. He knew that absence did not make the heart

31

grow fonder and for him to get his clutches into her, he had to make sure that the Friday lunch dates continued. "Well don't just give up on me like that, I know a great place we can have lunch today. Tell you what, I'll pick you up at eleven thirty sharp and surprise you with a lunch that will knock your socks off. I promise you will enjoy it and I will continue to be the perfect gentleman while I'm with you."

Cleo doodled on a pad as she listened to the excitement in his voice about his surprise lunch idea. Up to this point, she and Leonard had always met at Luggi's and when the lunch was over, she left and they went their separate ways. She knew she was really playing with fire if she agreed to get into his car and go to an unspecified place to have lunch. Intrigued by the thought of something different made her think twice, maybe there was no harm in him picking her up.

"Ok, I'll be outside of the hotel waiting for you at eleven thirty."

Leonard had the biggest grin in his face and could not hide his excitement when he said he would be outside her place of employment waiting for her at the specified time.

Standing outside his office door listening to his conversation was Sasha, the gum popping receptionist. "Who was that Leonard?" Sasha asked, standing in his doorway dressed like a hoochie mama in spiked heels, a sweater that left four inches of her midriff showing and a short leather skirt that fitted like a second layer of skin. "Did I hear you say you were picking her up for lunch and taking her someplace special?"

"Listen Sasha, I have business associates that I have to meet for lunch from time to time. Don't start that jealousy thing with me today, you know that I'm working when I away from this office during the day and some of my business associates just happen to be women. Go back to

Cleopatra's New Attitude

work and we'll go out for drinks this evening, I just might take you to my place and give you that special attention you say you always crave."

Leonard's words were just what the young woman wanted to hear. She quickly dropped her accusations, and was purring like a kitten.

*   *   *

Stepping out of the hotel into the chilly wind blowing off the Mississippi River sent a shiver through Cleopatra. She wrapped her coat closer around her body and looked around for signs of Leonard. Just as she thought of stepping back into the hotel to escape the cold, a black limousine pulled to the curb and out popped Leonard holding roses in his arms. Cleo was surprised but was grinning from ear to ear. She never expected to be picked up for lunch in such a grand fashion. As she accepted the roses and stepped into the limo, she felt like a schoolgirl. Never in her life had someone showered her with so much attention and treated her like a queen.

Standing in the window of the hotel was Poopie, taking in the entire scene. He was now sure that Cleopatra was having an affair and would not rest until he knew who the mystery man was. It was not out of just being nosey that pushed him to the point of not being able to stand the idea that Cleopatra might be having an affair, it was the green eyed monster of jealousy that gave fuel to Poopie's fire and that alone could mean danger to Cleo.

Chapter 7

"Sugar Pie, Honey Bunch—I can't help myself . . . ."

As Cleo rode to her unknown lunch destination, Leonard presented her with a flute of champagne and a small tray of caviar on butter crackers. It completely blew her mind and she was enjoying every minute of it. The ride was smooth, the music coming from the speakers in the back of the limo was slow and enticing and Leonard was ever attentive. They made small talk as the car whizzed out of the city and headed down interstate 40 east. Leonard handed her the phone and asked her to call back to the hotel and tell them she would be out at least three hours because she had something she needed to take care of. Although she was leery of doing as he asked, she called anyway and decided to enjoy as much of this as she could. She was in a limo with a professional driver and going to lunch in broad daylight, what could happen to her under such circumstances.

As they passed through the countryside, Leonard and Cleopatra enjoyed the scenery along the road. They talked about what they wanted for the future and after listening to Leonard, Cleo realized that although he was a successful businessman there was something missing in his life. The more Leonard talked the more Cleo was convinced the missing piece in his life was a family. The absence of a man in the house when Leonard was growing up had made a huge impression on him about having children and not being there as a father for them. Cleo listened intently but was sadden when she thought about her own situation. There would never be children for her and she would never reveal that to Leonard. She justified her not telling him by thinking that it was none of his business and their relationship was only based on friendship, not one where intimate details of her life would ever be exchanged. Telling Leonard about her inability to have children would only open old wounds and then she would end up telling him about losing her baby and why she really got married in the first place. No, that was too much for her to talk about and she preferred to keep her little secret and unhappy past to herself.

The car finally pulled off in Jackson, Tennessee, they had been riding for about an hour. As the driver slowed down, Cleo noticed a quaint little village area with small stores and a restaurant called "Casey Jones". The restaurant must have been a popular spot because the parking lot was crowded and people were busy walking in and out of the small retail shops circling the square. She was amused that he would bring her to such a quaint little place. It was not a romantic place but one that probably had down home cooking with a southern flair.

"Leonard, how did you ever find this little place?" Cleo was peeping through the back window of the limo at the little Christmas Store in the corner of the strip mall. "Before we leave here, I must visit the Christmas Store, I have been collecting angels for my Christmas tree for years and would love to see if they have something different."

Cleopatra's New Attitude

Leonard, seeing that she was pleased with his selection of their lunch destination, told the driver to park near the Christmas Store and they would walk from there to the restaurant.

"I'm happy you like the area, I attended school here at Lane College and this has always been one of my favorite places. I have always been a train fanatic and Casey Jones Village was one of the places I could visit and spend hours going through the shops and picking up odds and ends for my miniature train collection."

"You never told me you had a train collection," laughed Cleopatra as she stepped out of the car. "Men with miniature train collections are still little boys who refuse to grow up. However, I find that quite charming and I also think we all carry over a little of our childhood into our adult life. I still collect Barbie dolls and every time a new collectible one is introduced, I have to have it.

Leonard stopped and stood in front of Cleo. He loved the way she laughed and teased him about his hobby of collecting trains. He had never felt so at ease with a woman before and just her mere presence gave him a feeling of calm and made him happy. He wondered as he watched her talk and laugh just how it would feel to kiss her lips and hold her in his arms.

"Leonard, are you listening to me? You seem to be in another world and you had such a strange look in your eyes. Maybe we had better eat first and shop later, you look as if you need food", laughed Cleopatra as she pulled at his arm. She playfully pulled him along as he laughed and pretended as if he didn't want to go. They looked like two kids pulling and tugging toward the restaurant.

As they entered the restaurant, a little old lady greeted them and asked Leonard if he and the "Little Missus" would like to sit in the smoking or non-smoking area. Leonard chuckled as he thought of Cleopatra being his "Missus" and the idea struck him that it would suit him just fine. She was growing on him by leaps and bounds and the Friday lunches had become something he anxiously awaited every week.

"Please seat us in the non-smoking section. My friend nor I smoke and we would like to enjoy our lunch without having someone with a cigarette blowing smoke in our direction." Leonard then took Cleopatra's arm and led her behind the waitress. *I wonder if we look like a couple*, he thought. *We do look good together if I say so myself.* Making their way to the table, Leonard noticed people staring at them. His first impression was that people were thinking what a striking couple they made, his next thought was his needed to get as close to Cleopatra as he could and soon.

The menu at the restaurant was indeed down home southern cooking. Griddlecakes were being fried in the open and the buffet consisted of beans, greens, candied yams, okra and all the country fixings. Cleo and Leonard enjoyed every minute of their lunch and talked about their likes and dislikes while eating. Leonard was getting another view of the woman he had become strongly attracted to just by looking at her. He soon realized that she was a complex woman, but was the type of person with many friends and was loyal to friends and family.

After the meal, Leonard helped Cleo with her coat and as she turned around, he quickly grabbed her and pulled her to him. Before she knew it, Leonard had very gently started kissing her in the middle of the restaurant. It was not a forceful kiss, but one full of passion and ever so sensual. Her first reaction was to pull away and run to the nearest exit. Her second reaction was to receive the kiss and as she settled into his arms, she realized that she was enjoying it and could feel butterflies in her stomach.

Cleopatra's New Attitude

"I'm sorry Cleo," Leonard said in a breathy voice, "I should not have done that and I cannot explain to you why I did it. However, I can't say that I regret it. You do things to me and make me feel emotions that I should not be feeling."

"Don't apologize, I'm just as much at fault. Maybe we should cool it for a while and not see each other. I don't want our friendship to go sour on us because of a kiss, let's just forget this ever happened."

Forgetting that kiss ever happened would be hard for both of them. On the ride back home Cleo talked with a nervous chatter while Leonard sat and nodded his head. He was again having feelings that were frightening to him. She was starting to invade his very being and that kiss only told him what he knew was true—he had fallen in love with a married woman!

CHAPTER 8

"You've been cheatin . . . ."

Absence does not make the heart grow fonder, that is something Cleopatra knew to be true. So to get a grip on her situation with Leonard and to make sure that she did not let him cross the line again, she decided not to see him for a while. However, Leonard had other ideas about the absence of Cleo in his life. He could not get the woman out of his head and try as he would his thoughts were constantly about her.

Cleopatra and her girlfriends, who playfully called themselves "The Golden Girls", were always discussing and raking some man over the coals during their monthly meeting of their Sister-2-Sister club. Annette Hunter, the oldest of the group, was always the one to start the conversation about the "low life brothers" running around the city of Memphis trying to sniff out any woman who would give them some play. Pat Jackson would always defend the good "Christian brothers" who really got bad publicity because of the low down brothers. Kathy Lee, the youngest in the group and never married, would whine about her lack of companionship and how she had to be careful not to end up with a "man on the down low". And, Cleo was the instigator jumping from side to side defending the "low life brothers" because they never had love and attention in their young days, describing the "Christian brothers" as bible toting liars and the "down low brothers" as men who were just curious about other men because some woman had probably turned his ass out.

"The Golden Girls" began as a novel idea from a popular television show in the 1980's. The show was about a group of four retired women who lived together in a large house and shared each other's lives and ate cheesecake whenever there was a crisis. The gathering in the kitchen with coffee and cheesecake was the time when they hashed out their problems and confided in each other. One woman in the group (Claire) was the party girl, another was the sweet goofy girl (Rose), there was the tall woman (Maude) always looking for love and her mother (Sophia) who would say anything and constantly embarrassed her daughter and the others. Cleo and her friends often related to the antics pulled by each of the women and decided early on that they would pool their resources together when they were older and live together as "The Golden Girls".

Pat Jackson was the little feisty one in the group (Sophia). Not quite five feet tall, she made up for her small statue by being energetic and always butting into the lives of her friends. She had been married twice and had grown children who lived in other states so she had plenty of time to try to dictate to her friends just how they needed to run their lives. If any of them needed a shoulder to cry on, it was Pat they would run to and tell their troubles. Most of the time they would eventually regret telling her. Once she got her hands into their business, she was like a tiger and would not let go. Her mothering instinct took over and she played her role very well.

Cleopatra's New Attitude

Annette Hunter was the tall one in the group (Maude). Standing almost six feet tall she had a presence about her that people always noticed. She dressed in clothes that were stylish just as Maude did and she had a live and let live attitude. Divorced and having grown children, gave Annette all the freedom she needed. Her dating skills should have been written in a "how to" book for every woman to read. Always careful not to judge anyone but the first to stand up and tell others to mind their own business made Annette a special woman.

Kathy Lee (Claire) was the baby in the bunch. She was often referred to by men as a "brick house" because she was tall and every curve on her body was in the right place. She had never married and was quick to love a man and leave him to move on to another man if it suited her. She rightfully earned the title of heartbreaker as she left man after man heartbroken when she moved on to better territory. Although Pat and the others always tried to keep her under their wings and tell her to settle down, they knew it was her nature to be on the prowl and enjoy every minute of it.

Cleo decided long ago she had to be the "Rose" in the group. She didn't consider herself as goofy as Rose, but she could identify with some of the antics the woman pulled on the show. Rose was always the one to come up with a story to coincide with every deed the other's did.

The monthly meeting of the girls was one they always looked forward to having. It was a time they could laugh and hoot about any and everything while sitting in the kitchen drinking coffee and having cake—usually cheesecake. There was not a subject that was taboo and whatever they discussed stayed between the four of them.

Today Cleo was unusually quiet. Pat immediately noticed the somberness of her friend and knew something was bothering her. "Cleo, why the faraway look on your face today? Has something happened that you haven't told us about?"

Cleo looked over at Pat and smiled, *Damn, you can't keep anything from her*, she thought, *my face must be an open book*. "Well to be honest, there is something bothering me and I think I need to discuss it with the three of you."

Cleo begin to tell about her encounters with Leonard and how everything started with the mysterious gifts arriving at her office. The women listened intently with slightly amused looks on their faces. Cleo finished her story with the kiss that took place at the restaurant and her decision to put some distance between her and Leonard. When she finished, the room was as quiet as a cemetery, no one said a word and just sat and stared at her as if they were in shock.

Annette started applauding and the three women began giving Cleo high fives.

Pat was the first to speak, "Ok girlfriend, we need to talk and we need to talk in detail as a group. I think you need a little guidance on this subject. I told you some time ago to axe his ass and tell Michael what was happening. But, since you didn't follow that advice, let's come up with something else. The old fable you can't have your cake and eat it too does not apply to 'The Golden Girls'. I know about Leonard Wilkins' escapades and how he will use and lose a woman at the drop of a hat. I think you may have a hook in his nose and he needs to be reeled in. He has gone that extra mile with you and whether he knows it or not, you now have the upper hand"

"You can't be saying what I think you're saying", exclaimed Annette. "Because if you are, I think we can just have a little fun with one Mr. Wilkins."

The group wanted to know every detail of Cleo's encounters with Leonard. The fact that he had approached her during the charity event with his out of line remarks and because he had total disregard that her husband was accompanying her at the time made the women more vicious than they usually were. They chastised Cleo for letting the "friendship" go on for so long but told her they could understand how the attention he lavished on her would make her do what she did. Hell, they all would have probably done the same thing. You only live once and if some fool wanted to spend his money on you and not get anything in return he was dubbed the sucker. Cleo was having mixed feelings about the conversation and her friends wanting her to teach him a lesson. She knew that she could not let Leonard get any closer to her because her marriage to Michael was going to stay intact and getting intimate with another man was not something she would do.

Kathy was not participating in the plotting as much as Pat and Annette. Cleo immediately sensed she was not telling something and that her mind had wandered to another time and place.

Reaching over and touching her friend's hand Cleo leaned toward her, "Kathy, are you listening to us? What are you thinking about that could be more important than what we're talking about?"

"Well girls, I know something I think I should tell before we finish this plotting."

Kathy went on to tell the women about a young woman she knew who once worked with her. The woman had been dating Leonard for

Mercedes M. Alexander

almost a year when she began to get phone calls and letters from other women threatening her and telling her she had better stay away from him. Her tires were slashed at her apartment complex, lipstick was used to write nasty messages on her car two or three times and one of the women actually confronted her and threatened to do bodily harm if she didn't stay away from Leonard Wilkins. Every time the young woman approached Leonard to talk about the incidents, he was able to convince her there was nothing to the women and they were jealous because he had chosen her over them and the other women were just "supportive friends". This went on for months and finally the girl decided to hire a private detective to follow Leonard for a period of six weeks to find out just what he did when he was not with her. The report from the private investigator made the girl physically ill. It seems that Leonard was stringing along four women at the same time, while he wined and dined them on an equal basis. The investigator told her all four of them had identical gifts he had lavished on them and when he sent flowers, the florist made four deliveries and each time there were three dozen roses in different colors. The young lady finally ended the relationship but not before she discovered she had contacted a sexually transmitted disease. Luckily, for her, it was something that could be cleared up with antibiotics. She gave Leonard's name to the health department officials as the only man she had been sleeping with and went immediately to his office to confront him. Her first surprise was to find one of the women working in his office and her second surprise was that he tried to tell her that he had been very good to her and she should not be upset with him because he had never promised her anything. Her gut feeling was that he was trying to keep himself in the clear with his woman working in the office while quietly dismissing her. After she had had a

Cleopatra's New Attitude

few words with him, she calmly went back to her car and took a baseball bat out of the trunk and proceeded to wreck everything in her path in his office. She eventually had her job transferred to another city and Kathy had not heard anything from her in a few years. Kathy also referred to him as a sexual predator because the women were always much younger.

Mouths dropped at Kathy's revelation, nobody could believe that any one man could be that calculating and such a user. This knowledge alone helped to make up Cleopatra's mind that Mr. Leonard Wilkins needed to be taught a lesson and she would be the one to do it with the help of her friends. She had no doubt in her mind he was playing her too and was trying to get her to the point that he could take control and make her one of his many sexual conquests.

The plotting began and the monthly meeting of the Sister-2-Sister club ended up being a four-hour meeting where the wine flowed freely and the viciousness of a group of women was laid out in a plan of action. This plan was one that was cold and calculated and any human man would not survive it with his dignity still intact.

CHAPTER 9

"It's all in the game . . . ."

While sitting at his desk in his enormous and well-appointed office, Leonard could not concentrate on his work. His mind kept floating off in fantasyland to a place where there was only him and Cleopatra Beavers. This woman had gotten under his skin in a way that no woman ever had. When he walked in the rain he thought about her, if he smelled any type of pleasant fragrance he thought about her, before he closed his eyes at night he wondered what she was doing and while he slept he dreamed of her. He had to laugh at himself, he was thoroughly whipped and had not even been intimate with the woman. He also wondered if and when the opportunity arose, would he be able to hold her in his arms and make passionate love to her without losing his cool. He had never waited so long for any woman. They usually dropped their panties within a few weeks of his wooing but this woman was different. She was not to be bought, was not easily impressed and was very much in control. Leonard's worry now was how much she had controlled him and how he had loved every minute of it.

Now, Cleo had drawn a line and wanted the relationship to cool for a few weeks. She had told him that both of them needed to get their heads on straight and realize that this could not go farther than friendship. Her firm tone of voice about not sleeping around and being a one-man woman shook him to his core. He then realized that he may never have this woman and the more he realized her stance on being faithful to one man, the more he wanted her and nobody but her. His thoughts were interrupted by the buzz on his phone.

"Yes Sasha".

Sasha, smacking gum into the phone in her usual lazy tone said, "There's a Miss Kathy Lee here to see you, she said she is with some charity and wanted to talk with you about a donation."

"Please tell her that I'm busy right now and to leave a card."

"I already tried that and she said you will see her and you'll see her today."

Well who in the hell could this be? thought Leonard. "Alright have her come in Sasha."

As Leonard looked up he saw Sasha leading a woman around 35 years old who was dressed to the nines. Her gorgeous long hair had light brown streaks and surrounded her face in an enticing way. She had legs that were long and shapely with a little tiny waist that gave additional emphasis to her bust line. Her walk was seductive and she had an air of sophistication that made you take a second look at her. His first thought was "wow"!

Kathy sauntered into the room knowing she had the man's full attention and extended her hand to Leonard. She looked him dead in the eye and gave him one of her "I'm available" looks, a look she knew he could not resist. When he asked her to take a seat, she immediately did so and crossed her legs ever so seductively. Leonard's eyes were about to pop out of his head and his dog attitude moved into bow-wow mode taking over his senses.

Cleopatra's New Attitude

"Well Ms. Lee, just what can I can do for you today," said Leonard with a gleam in his eyes.

"Thank you for taking the time to talk with me Mr. Wilkins. I won't take much of your time but I wanted to ask if you would be kind enough to give a donation to the building of our church daycare center. Our church is small but the need for childcare in the area where we are located is great and the mothers are welfare recipients who cannot afford to pay much for childcare while working the meager paying jobs the government has provided. We are in the process of getting non-profit status for the center and government funding, but that will take a while and we need to make this service available to these mothers as soon as possible. Can we count on you to help us financially with a onetime donation?"

"Well, Miss Lee—it is Miss Lee isn't it?"

"Yes, it's Miss, I've never been married and I'm pretty much new to this area and got involved in church as soon as I moved here, that's why I'm out soliciting financial aid for this worthy cause." Kathy batted her eyes while slowly reeling the fool into her web.

"I would love to donate something to your cause Miss Lee" . . . .

"Oh, please call me Kathy, it's more friendly and not as cold."

Leonard straightened his back and cleared his throat. "Well, Kathy it is. I think we should discuss this away from my office. Are you available for dinner this evening, I think we can get into more detail about your daycare center's needs and just what I might be able to do to help."

The fool is taking the bait, thought Kathy, *now all I have to do is play along and pretty soon this playa is going to be played and put in his place.* "Dinner sounds great to me, what time and where should I meet you."

"Let's say around seven at the "Isaac Hayes Restaurant". Are you familiar with that area?"

"Oh yes, I know exactly where that's located, I'll be there at seven sharp". With that being said, Kathy rose from the chair and strutted out of the room but not before she turned to give him another one of her come-on smiles.

I'll just be damn, how lucky can I get, thought Leonard as he sat back behind his desk. He could smell a conquest coming and would enjoy every bit of it with that "little hotty".

Rushing to finish his task at hand, Leonard called Sasha and told her not to send any more calls to him and that he would be leaving the office early. The chase was on and Leonard was being his old self, licking his lips while thinking just what he would do with Miss Kathy Lee as soon as he dropped his killer charm on her. You could smell the "bow-wow" scent coming from every pore in his body.

*   *   *

At six thirty sharp, Cleo, Pat and Annette met at the front of the Isaac Hayes Restaurant and asked, while being ushered in by the waiter, to be seated at the back table that was not very visible to other customers in the restaurant. The plan was for Kathy to arrive fifteen minutes earlier than Leonard and ask for the table near the front by the window. This would put Kathy and Leonard in an area where they could not see the three women but could be observed by them.

Kathy arrived as scheduled and was seated. She was wearing her "Delilah" dress, it was cut so low in the front even a priest would have been tempted. She had dressed just the way she knew would get Leonard's full attention and have him salivating. Less than ten minutes later Leonard arrived carrying three dozen yellow roses, his eyes immediately went toward the low cut bust line in her dress. Once she noticed the placement of his eyes staring directly at her bosom, she knew she had him.

That bastard, thought Cleopatra. *I was starting to feel we might be going too far with this plan, but now I'll just let the shit hit the fan and fly wherever it wants. He deserves to get his ass caught in a sling and I hope he chokes to death before the evening ends.*

For more than an hour the women discretely watched Leonard smile and try to impress Kathy. Then Annette announced it was time to take the plan to step two.

Cleopatra had worn a slinky animal print dress with matching cork wedge shoes. When she moved every man in the restaurant turned and looked her way. She slowly walked up to the booth where Leonard and Kathy sat. Leonard had long ago left his side of the booth and planted himself beside Kathy. His back was turned to Cleopatra and he did not see her as she approached the booth.

Cleo slid in on the opposite side if the booth just in time to hear Leonard run his famous line "you ought to let me hit it" by Kathy.

"Well, fancy meeting you here Leonard. I was having dinner with my girlfriends and spotted you sitting here with this cute young thing. Is this your niece or some other relative?" And do you always ask women to let you, as you put it "hit it" while begging for sex on the sly?"

Leonard, in total shock, bit his tongue as he chewed the last of his steak and could not speak for a few moments. This gave Kathy the chance

Mercedes M. Alexander

to jump in and answer Cleo's question. In her most bitchy tone she piped, "No, I'm not a relative and just who the hell are you?"

"I'm just a nobody, I'm the last woman he tried to woo but he never made it to second base. It seems that he didn't suffer over me too long, it's only been a couple of weeks and he's out doing his usual thing again."

The feeling Leonard was having at this moment was not a good one. The last person he wanted to see him out with another woman was Cleopatra. He was caught and had nowhere to turn.

"Hello, Cleopatra." Let me introduce you to Ms. Kathy Lee. Kathy this is my friend, Cleopatra Beavers."

The two women sat and stared each other down. If you were an observer from another table you would have been quick to believe that a catfight was about to ensue. Kathy and Cleopatra were playing this scene perfectly and Leonard was as nervous as a straight man in a gay club.

"I met Kathy this afternoon in my office, she asked me to donate to a project at her church and we were just discussing what I could do in terms of helping".

"It looks to me like you had more than discussing the terms of a deal on your mind and just what the hell are you doing buying yellow roses for a woman you claim you just met this evening. From where I was sitting it looked as if you were ready to run your hand up this whore's dress and get your old fart jollies on by feeling her up."

Leonard was mortified, he had nowhere to turn and saw that Cleo was slowly rising to come around the booth and Kathy was trying to stand to meet her coming. Leonard was right smack in the middle and was nervous about the two of them getting any closer so he stood to be a buffer between the women.

Cleopatra's New Attitude

As Cleo rounded the booth she picked up Leonard's dessert of blackberry cobbler with ice cream and Kathy picked up her dessert of apple pie with ice cream. The two women took aim simultaneously and threw the dishes. Both of the desserts landed on each side of Leonard's head. It took all she had in her not to giggle when she saw the look on his face, but by now anger had taken over and Cleopatra was going to play this one through. Kathy did have to lower her head to keep from laughing aloud but quickly regain her composure and began wiping Leonard's head with her napkin.

"Oh you poor baby, just look what that bitch made me do," quipped Kathy as she wiped her napkin through the gooey dessert. "I am so sorry Leonard, here let me help you."

As Kathy wiped his face on one side, smearing the mess along the back of Leonard's expensive Italian made suit, Cleopatra picked up another napkin and began smearing the dessert on the front of his suit.

With tears in her eyes Cleopatra said, "I can't believe you would push me aside so quickly Leonard, I truly believed that I really meant something to you and had decided to call. I can't tell you how much you have hurt me."

That being said Cleopatra walked quickly outside the restaurant with Leonard running after her. Before he could catch her, she had gotten in the back of Annette's waiting car and was quickly driven from the scene. The three women laughed until they cried at the sight of Leonard standing in the middle of the street looking like he had fallen in the ice cream vat at Willy Wonka's Factory.

*   *   *

Mercedes M. Alexander

Later that night, the four women met at Pat's house and started plans for the next show down. They were more than pleased about the performance that was given during dinner and were anxious to keep the ball rolling.

While the women were talking back and forth about the next step to be taken, Kathy congratulated Cleo on her performance.

"Girl, that last statement about being hurt and the make believe tears you had in your eyes should get you a nomination for an Academy Award."

The statement made by Kathy caused Cleo to stop and think. Deep in her heart she wondered if it really was an act, the tears came too easy and there was an emotion she was feeling that made her so sad. All the while Cleo was thinking, Pat kept a carefully trained eye on her friend, she knew that it was not all an act.

Kathy told them Leonard had come back into the restaurant and paid the waiter without saying a word to her. He then walked out and never looked back.

CHAPTER 10

"Just to be close to you . . . ."

'You reap what you sow', was the thought running through Leonard's mind as he closed himself up in his house for the day. It was a Saturday morning and he would usually be out and about town on a beautiful day such as this. But today Leonard was having a private pity party. He was embarrassed that his shit was so ragged and he would be caught by one woman while wooing another. Never in his days of playing the field had anything like this ever happened to him. He was really devastated that Cleopatra was the one to catch him in the act of cheating. Although he really wasn't cheating, because he had not reached the level with Cleopatra that would constitute an intimate relationship between a man and a woman. But the look on her face when she said he had hurt her crushed his heart. The last thing he ever wanted to do was to hurt her, his only wish was to be her everything. Of all the women he had ever messed around with, the one he cared for the most would be the one to catch him in the act. Maybe God was trying to tell him something. Whatever the matter, Leonard had to come up with something to get Cleopatra back in

Mercedes M. Alexander

his life. He would not let this small incident keep him from the woman he really wanted to be by his side, husband or no husband.

'*What the hell am I doing*', thought Leonard as he stood in the middle of his kitchen pouring yet another drink of straight gin. He had not taken a bath, shaved or eaten anything all day. He quickly put the shot glass back on the counter and made a beeline to the bathroom to get cleaned up. He would make an appearance tomorrow and see Cleopatra come hell or high water. Seeing her again was the only thing that would ease his troubled mind.

*   *   *

Sitting in the choir stand listening to the preacher saying to forgive your enemies made Cleo feet a little guilty about her activities during the past seventy-two hours. When the preacher opened the doors of the church and asked that she sing one of his favorite songs, she slowly made her way to the microphone. As she sang, she looked into the audience and noticed Kathy standing in her usual position as head usher and pointing down the aisle a few rows ahead of where she was standing. Cleopatra really got into her song and ignored Kathy. It was not until she made her way back to her seat that she noticed exactly what Kathy wanted her to see. There sitting on the tenth row near the middle isle was none other than Leonard Wilkins. Cleo almost swallowed her tongue, just what did he mean by invading her private territory and coming to her church knowing it would make her feel uncomfortable. Did he come for a showdown? Whatever the reason, Cleopatra braced herself for an unpleasant afternoon.

As soon as church was dismissed, Cleopatra slipped through the back door and sent one of the members to tell Michael she would be waiting in the car.

Leonard was straining his neck looking for Cleo, she was nowhere to be found. He was a little disappointed that he did not get a chance to talk with her. But hearing her sing was more than he could have asked for. As she stood there singing, he felt as if God had lifted a burden from him. Surely, someone who could sing like an angel could not hold a grudge for long. His only thought was seeing her face to face as soon as possible so that he could beg for her forgiveness.

Leaving the church, he turned to see a woman walking quickly away from him. His first thought was that it was Kathy the young lady who was the cause of all his present problems. He immediately dismissed the thought, he surmised that it must be his guilty conscience playing tricks on him.

*　　*　　*

When Cleopatra arrived at work on Monday morning, sitting on her desk at 8:30 a.m. were 12 vases of multi-colored roses. She did not bother to open any of the cards and quickly took them and stuck them in her desk. She then proceeded to place a vase of roses on each one of the desks of her fellow women co-workers. The last vase was taken and put on the desk of Poopie.

There, that ought to make the little fairy happy. At least he has the same thing as all of the other women in the office and he has not been discriminated against, was the thought running through Cleo's mind as she chuckled.

With her task finished, she quickly returned to her desk before her co-workers began arriving for their 9 to 5 work shift.

The women in the office were ecstatic when they arrived and saw flower arrangements on their desk. They immediately noticed that Cleopatra was the only woman without flowers. Two of them immediately inquired as to why she didn't have flowers and she quickly replied and said she received flowers but had put them on Poopie's desk so that he would not feel left out.

"Child that was real nice of you but I would have died and gone to hell before I gave up my roses to Ms. Thang", was the first thing out of Rose Smith's mouth.

"Oh, I didn't mind," replied Cleopatra. "I know that he will appreciate them and I wanted to do something to make him happy. We all know that he's been down in the dumps since his last friend left him for somebody else, maybe this will perk him up for a little while."

No sooner had Cleo spoken those words Poopie switched into the office. He immediately started jerking his head from side to side in a most dramatic fashion as he looked from desk to desk at the beautiful roses. When he looked over at Cleo's desk and saw nothing he immediately had a puzzled look on his face but made no comment. As he entered his office he let out a little scream and could be heard all over the office crying about how nice it was that someone thought of him.

As the day wore on, Cleopatra busied herself with one task after another. She remembered to take the cards from the roses out of her desk drawer and slid them into her purse. Just as she was doing so, up popped Ms. Poopie. He never said a word but gave her a knowing nod and a smile.

Cleopatra's New Attitude

At twelve sharp, Cleopatra got up from her desk and decided to walk down the street to a local deli and get a light lunch. As she exited the building she was approached by Leonard. She was upset with herself because her first reaction was that she was happy to see him. That reaction was quickly squelched and she turned to face him with a frown on her face.

"Before you go off on me and walk away, please let me talk to you. I need to see you Cleopatra, I can't tell you what I've been through these last few days. Please just talk to me".

"I have nothing to say to you Leonard, now please stay away from me and don't bother sending me anymore flowers". Cleo then crossed the street and walked away from Leonard. Plan two would now be put into place and she had him just where her friends told her he would be.

After Cleo settled herself into her seat at the deli and had given the waiter her order she reached into her purse and pulled out the 12 cards that had been attached to the roses. The first one read "I beg for your forgiveness, I promise to never hurt you again", the second card had the same reading and so did all the rest until she came to card number 12. The last card read, "Cleopatra, my queen, I think I am in love for the first time and I only have love for you." She was startled by the last card and could not believe the audacity of this man trying to use the word love to get her to forgive him.

*   *   *

Leonard walked back to his car and was truly upset. He would not let this woman get away from him, he had to have her.

Arriving back at his office, Leonard noticed Sasha was in a foul mood. The florist had called and wanted to confirm they had delivered twelve dozen roses in separate vases to a Ms. Cleopatra Beavers. Sasha slammed the phone back into its receiver and sat quietly waiting for her boss/lover.

"Who the hell is Cleopatra Beavers and what do you mean by sending her twelve dozen roses. Isn't that the bitch who called weeks ago and you gave me some bullshit about her being a client?"

Leonard was angry with the young woman attacking Cleopatra and was not about to let her get away with it.

"Sasha, I will remind you one more time that you are an employee in this office and you are not to snoop around in my private business affairs. Furthermore, as long as your ass is black, you are to never refer to Ms. Beavers as a bitch. Do you understand me?"

After chastising his young secretary, he walked to his office and slammed the door. His other employees huddled together and snickered about Leonard snatching Sasha down from her perch and putting her in her place. However, Sasha was now very angry and decided that "Ms. Beavers" had to go and she would do whatever was necessary to keep her away from Leonard who was not only her boss, but also a very generous sugar daddy.

Chapter 11

"Heavy fallin' out . . . ."

Michael Beavers noticed that his wife had not been in a cheery mood for the last few weeks. He did whatever he could to make her smile and bring the old Cleopatra back but nothing he did seemed to work. He had been working hard for the last few months trying to help with a group of young men at the school who were in desperate need of a strong man to be a role model. Because of his extra activities and Cleopatra's mood he had paid very little attention to the slight tightening he was having in his chest. Visiting a doctor's office was not something he did unless it was his last recourse and this little pain did not warrant a doctor's visit.

"Hi sugar, how was your day".

Cleo looked up as she walked into the house and forced a smile on her face as she flopped on the living room sofa. "It was the usual, people coming and going while business moves on. I can't complain because I really love my job."

Michael walked around the sofa, took Cleo's shoes from her feet, placed her feet on the ottoman and began massaging his wife's shoulders.

Mercedes M. Alexander

"I've been thinking Cleo, we have both been working hard and we need to take some time off and just get away. In a few months school will be out for a week for spring break and I want you to see if you can take the week off during that time. I would like to go on a vacation and maybe take a cruise."

Cleopatra was thrilled. Michael had never suggested that they take time off for a vacation in their many years of marriage. His suggestion could not have come at a better time and maybe taking a romantic vacation with her husband would take her mind off Leonard.

"I would love to take a cruise and I can call the travel agent tomorrow to see what is available at that time."

"Good, then you go ahead and plan one and I'll go wherever you want. I think we both need some down time and getting away where we can't be reached will be good for both of us".

Cleopatra was happy and could not wait until morning to contact the travel agency. She really needed to get away and a cruise was something Michael had been promising her for the last fifteen years and had never done.

*   *   *

On Wednesday of that week, the Golden Girls all met for drinks after work. Their favorite place was a little club on Beale Street that served free appetizers during what they called "business after hours". The atmosphere was good and the people were all familiar to the group. They would sit and talk then mingle with some of the other people.

Cleopatra's New Attitude

This evening would be very different for "the Golden Girls." Leonard had been coaxed by Sasha to take her out for drinks after work. She walked into the club with her arms entwined with Leonard's trying to make her entrance and be noticed on the arm of Memphis' most eligible bachelor. The place was packed and Leonard never noticed the group of four women watching him and his secretary as they made their rounds greeting people. When the music started the first thing Sasha did was pull Leonard to the dance floor and slowly did a seductive grind on him while he basically stood still.

"My God, that's got to be the most degrading thing I've seen a woman do in a long time. She's almost screwing him right there on the dance floor!" Annette was livid at the display of disregard Sasha had for the other women in the place and the total lack of respect for herself.

Kathy was straining her eyes to get a closer look at the woman. "My, my, that's the wench who works in his office. She gave me the look over a couple of times while I was sitting out in the waiting area before I went into Leonard Wilkins' office. My first impression was that she did not like the fact that he closed the door and put her in a position so that she did not know what was going on in his office. When I left the office, she took extra efforts to be nice to me and tried to do a little girl-to-girl talk. Her only point was to let me know that he had bought her a little raggedy ass watch with diamond accents and how generous he was by sending her to secretarial school." Kathy laughed as she thought of the scene in his office. "He should have sent the uncouth heifer to charm school."

All of the women roared at Kathy's last statement. Seeing how the woman was dressed, and the show she was putting on as she danced, gave all of them the impression that Leonard loved dealing with trash.

Mercedes M. Alexander

"From what I've heard, and now from what I've seen, that must be the type of hoochie he enjoys", stated Pat. "He ought to be ashamed of himself".

Cleo slowly turned to continue to watch the display on the dance floor that had caught everybody's attention. When she saw Leonard just standing there and letting the woman grind him as if she were a prostitute, she felt as if she would throw up. Quickly excusing herself from the table, she headed toward the ladies restroom. As she walked past the dance floor someone she knew called out her name.

"Hey Cleopatra, stop by our table on your way back. We want to discuss something with you about room rentals at the Marriott."

Cleo turned and nodded her head while hurrying past them. She could feel the bowel rising in her throat and did not dare stop to talk with anyone.

While entertaining the crowd doing her thing on the dance floor, Sasha heard the man call out Cleo's name and watched her intently as she headed toward the ladies room. "I'll be right back baby", she told Leonard as she made a quick exit from the dance floor and a beeline to the ladies room.

Cleopatra stood in the stall and emptied her stomach. Her head was spinning and she braced herself against the wall hoping the nausea would quickly pass. After she left the stall and was standing to rinse her mouth out at the sink, she looked up in the mirror and the woman who had entertained the crowd on the dance floor appeared right behind her.

"Excuse me, but is your name Cleopatra Beavers?"

"Yes it is—do I know you or is there something I can do for you?"

"Yeah, there's plenty you can do for me. You can leave my man alone and take your high and mighty ass someplace else. Leonard Wilkins is

Cleopatra's New Attitude

mine and I'm not letting you or anybody else have him. I don't want you talking to him, calling him or seeing him at any time. He's mine and you need to back off!"

Turning to face the obstinate heifer, Cleo pushed her aside and immediately told her she could have the son of a bitch because the two of them probably deserved each other. As she walked out the door to join her friends, Sasha followed her closely cursing the entire time.

Leonard was horrified as he heard Sasha screaming and calling someone all types of bitches. He immediately saw Cleopatra as she headed his way with Sasha in close pursuit. As Cleo came near him, she only glared at him and kept walking to the table where her friends were now standing up and ready to do a quick throw down with the little twit trying to harass their friend.

Before Annette, Pat and Kathy could push Cleopatra aside and grab Sasha, Leonard pushed her toward the door and out of the club. Never in his life had he had a woman embarrass him in front of so many people and it was now time for Sasha to pack her things and get out of his life. Had she attacked any other woman, Leonard might have laughed about it and enjoyed seeing two women fighting over him. But Sasha had approached the wrong woman and Leonard was not having any of it. Nobody would ever attacked Cleopatra and not have to deal with him. He might have to love her from afar but love her he would, and men always protected women they truly loved.

Sitting in the corner of the club close to the ladies restroom and taking in the entire scene was Poopie. He was putting two and two together. The card out of the Gucci wallet had the initials of L.W. and the man Sasha had verbally attacked Cleopatra over was none other than Leonard

Wilkins, the man most women in the city of Memphis drooled over. It occurred to him that the man was drooling over Cleo and most likely was the bearer of all the flowers and gifts. Whatever the situation, Poopie had Cleopatra's back. She had proven to him that she was his friend and he was not about to let anything happen to her.

As Cleo and her friends left the club, there were no words passed among them. They were all fighting mad and revenge was all they wanted. How dare Leonard Wilkins bring his hoochie to their local turf and what had he told her about Cleo that would make her attack her the way she had. The saying that there is nothing worse than the wrath of a woman scorned was created just for this situation. The wrath of three of the Golden Girls was something Leonard would experience on behalf of their friend.

*　　*　　*

The next morning in Leonard's office was nothing short of major chaos. He stood over Sasha while she cried and packed her belongings. He had called the accountant during the night and told him to come to work early and cut a severance check for Sasha. The accountant was more than happy come to work early to do his boss' bidding and made calls to everybody else on staff that night to let them know that Sasha was being given the boot. All of the employees came to work early that day so they could witness with glee the defrocking of one Sasha Lewis.

CHAPTER 12

"Smoke Gets In Your Eyes . . . ."

A few months passed and spring was arriving with the usual heavy rains and the blooming of flowers. Because of the beautiful weather, people were venturing out in the city parks and on the riverbanks of Memphis. As Cleopatra sat in the park across from her office during one of her breaks, she watched the lovers in the park holding hands and kissing in public. She absent mindedly thought of Leonard and the kiss in the restaurant. How could she have been so stupid and naïve, she was a grown ass woman acting like a silly school girl taking chances she could not afford to take. Cleopatra had not seen Leonard since that dreadful encounter she had with his girlfriend and she had no intentions of ever seeing him again.

Leonard, during all of this time, had decided to give Cleo a cooling down period. Staying away from her for almost three months was torture for him but he knew she needed her space. He kept himself busy with new projects and tried to steer clear of all women. However, the women in the city of Memphis did not have that same idea. The knowledge floating around town that he was not attached to any woman made him more enticing to them and they were on the chase. Leonard was turning down

Mercedes M. Alexander

blatant proposals constantly, he could not believe the gall of some of the women approaching him. One of his most frequent visitors was a woman who was a friend of his ex-wife. The word within their group of friends was that she actually told Leonard's ex-wife to leave him and not put up with his screwing all around town. Now that some time had passed, this woman decided it was time to make her move. She had been plotting all the time and getting rid of Leonard's wife was the beginning.

*   *   *

The other three Golden Girls were still holding their grudges and were trying to find the perfect plot to put the man they now described as the "dog of dogs" in his place. Every idea they came up with did not do enough justice to the man and they were determined to have the last laugh on Leonard.

Cleopatra and her husband, Michael, were concentrating on their upcoming cruise and planning to have a relaxing time while visiting the Virgin Islands. They had decided to fly to St. Croix and spend three days and catch the cruise ship from that point for a four day cruise to two other islands and then home. Cleo had packed and re-packed her clothes, not really knowing what she wanted to take with her. She was torn between the idea of just taking things to relax in and not worry about attending anything that would require her to dress-up. In the end, she made the decision to take a few party clothes just in case there was something special on the ship she and Michael would want to attend.

*   *   *

Cleopatra and Michael enjoyed their vacation immensely. The island hospitality extended to them in St. Croix was more than they had expected. They toured the old plantations and were amazed at the history such a small island had. The tour of the Rum Factory was their favorite. They were able to sample just about every flavor of rum imaginable to man. The tropical gardens, beaches and old forts were also highlights of their stay and they took pictures to remind them of their visit.

During the last day of their stay on the island, Michael presented Cleopatra with a Cruzan bracelet encrusted with five small diamonds. He explained to her that if her heart was taken, she was to wear the bracelet with the hook pointing toward the heart. It was one of the most beautiful things she had seen and brought tears to her eyes. To show her love for Michael, Cleo made a special trip to the same jewelers and purchased a silver Cruzan bracelet with a gold hook attached for him.

That evening while packing to catch the ship the next morning, Cleo noticed Michael holding his chest and breathing deeply. When she questioned him about it, he told her he had been experiencing some heartburn and thought it was from some of the spicy island food. Although Cleo was concerned, she accepted his explanation and offered him Pepto-Bismol she had brought along for the trip. Michael quickly took the medication and within fifteen minutes told her that he was feeling fine.

The next morning as they boarded the cruise ship, Cleopatra was in for another surprise from Michael. They were escorted to a private cabin with its own balcony. It was one of the luxury cabins on the ship. Michael had called the travel agent and gotten an upgrade. His thoughtfulness was very touching to Cleopatra and added a new chapter to their love life. She

Mercedes M. Alexander

had never felt for him the way she felt during their vacation. There was a side to Michael he had never shown Cleopatra and she was seeing her husband for the first time as a giving, adoring man.

"Michael, I haven't been this happy in a long time. I think we needed to get away to find ourselves again. Hasn't this been the most wonderful few days?"

Michael looking over at his wife and wishing the moment could last forever grabbed her hand and kissed it. "Honey, I can't tell you how much I have enjoyed being here with you and being able to focus just on us. It seems we both have been living in our own separate worlds. I believe from this point on we will take extra efforts to make our marriage as magical as it has been since we arrived on the island."

Their experiences on the ship were more than they expected. Casinos, Las Vegas shows and spa experiences were a few of the many amenities on the ship. The four day cruise home seemed to fly by so quickly that Cleo and Michael promised each other this was something they would do every year. The time spent alone with her husband gave Cleo a clearer understanding of what she really needed to cherish—her marriage.

Two days after returning home from the cruise, Michael was still complaining of discomfort in his chest. On his way out of the front door heading to work on Wednesday following their vacation, Michael collapsed. Cleopatra, while backing her car out of the driveway, just happened to look up at the front door and saw Michael fall. She immediately stopped her car and ran to him. She could not get any response from him and dialed 911 from her cell to request an ambulance. On the ride to the hospital, she sat in the back of the ambulance praying silently that Michael would be all right. The paramedics were able to revive him for a short while and informed Cleo that he appeared to have had had a heart attack and the damage would not be known until they were able to get him into the hospital to run test.

Cleo called Michael's parents from the hospital telling them of Michael's illness and begging them to get there as soon as possible. Her second call was to Pat because she knew that she would inform everybody else and be there for moral support as soon as she could.

Cleopatra's prayers to God were asking him to heal Michael. They had just reached a point in their marriage where things were looking so much brighter and now this had to happen.

The family was informed by one of the physicians on duty that Michael would have to have a triple bypass and the surgical team was scrubbing up and waiting for Doctor Brian Brewer, who was one of the most highly skilled surgeons in his field.

After three hours the doctor finally came out of surgery to give Cleo and Michael's parents a report on his condition. The grim look on the physician's face made Cleo's heart stop while Michael's parents held on to her for support.

"Mrs. Beavers, I'm Doctor Brewer, the surgeon who performed the triple bypass on your husband. Did he have any warning signs before the actual heart attack happened? Usually in cases such as this, your husband would have been experiencing some chest pains and shortness of breath. Luckily, for him, he is physically strong and I believe he will be fine in a few months. He will need to be monitored by me for a while and will need to take medication to help with his heart. If you would like to see him, you as family can go in only two at a time and please make your visit short. I don't expect him to regain consciousness until tomorrow."

Mercedes M. Alexander

Cleo with tears streaming down her face reached over and hugged the doctor. "Thank you Doctor Brewer, I can't tell you how grateful I am that you were able to operate and repair Michael's heart. Please know that he will have the best of care and I will personally see to it that he does everything necessary to get him back on his feet."

Cleo stood back and let Michael's parents go in to visit him first. When they came out she went in alone and sat holding his hand and remembering his complaint of chest pains while on vacation and his apparent problem with his breathing. It made her wonder if he had been experiencing pain for some time and did not tell her. He had so many tubes running in and out of his body and appeared very frail to Cleo. As she sat beside him, she felt pangs of guilt because she did not recognize any symptoms of Michael having heart problems. She vowed then and there she would take care of him and make sure he had the best of care.

"Hi honey, I can't believe you're lying here with all these tubes running everywhere, less than a week after our vacation. Remember telling me we would have to take a vacation every year? Well, I'm going to hold you to that and in order for you to fulfill your promise, you must get well. I need you Michael, please come back to me."

Cleo thought she felt Michael squeeze her hand. She kissed his forehead and said goodnight to him as she quietly went out of the room.

CHAPTER 13

"The thrill is gone . . . ."

Michael's recuperation period was very slow. He was not responding to the medication as well as the doctors had expected. Cleopatra took a three month leave of absence from her job so that she could be home and give him the care he needed. The realization that Michael was not getting well as fast as he should kept Cleo stressed. Michael tried to be a good patient and keep a smile on his face but the fact that he did not bounce back to his old self as quickly as he thought he should made him a little testy at times. Cleo was very patient with him and did all she could to cheer him up and let him know that in time he would regain all his strength.

One morning during the third month of Michael's recuperation, Cleo was making lunch for him when the doorbell rang. When she answered the door, there stood before her a young woman no more than 24 years old. She was attractively dressed and had in her arms a beautiful little girl.

Cleo smiled at the adorable child and looked at the woman holding her. "Hello, may I help you?"

Mercedes M. Alexander

"Yes, I believe you can. My name is Paula Mims and this is my daughter Alexis. I recently returned to town and heard about Michael's illness and I decided to come by to introduce myself and let Michael see his little girl."

The air suddenly became very thick and Cleopatra thought she could not breath. She braced herself in the doorway and stared from the child to the mother. Did she hear what she thought she had heard? Was this woman insinuating Michael was the father of this child?

"I'm sorry, I don't believe I heard you correctly. Did you say this was my husband Michael's child?"

"Yes you heard me correctly, may I please come in and talk with you. I didn't come to make a scene, I just needed to get this out in the open. I thought it was time you knew about Alexis."

Cleo invited the woman in and asked her to take a seat in the living room. She quickly found out that Michael had been paying child support to the woman since the baby was born and because of him being sick the support checks had stopped. The young woman was at one time a student of Michael's and they had begun an affair three years ago after she finished college and returned home. When she found out she was pregnant, she refused to abort the baby. Michael insisted she have an abortion and gave her five thousand dollars. Paula had taken the money and left town to live with friends. After the baby was born, she returned to Memphis and insisted that Michael support the child. Michael had refused to have anything to do with her or the child until she threatened to tell Cleopatra. Now the baby was being raised by Paula's 80 year old grandmother and she needed the child support checks to make ends meet.

Cleopatra's New Attitude

"I'm so sorry Mrs. Beavers to drop this bomb on you. I've just started a good job in Chicago and don't have the time to raise a baby. My grandmother needs this money on a regular basis to take care of Alexis."

The two women sat and talked for thirty minutes. Cleopatra was numb throughout the entire conversation. She did not know what she was feeling, but she could not take her eyes off that adorable little girl. The child finally reached for Cleopatra and sat in her lap playing with her necklace while smiling and cooing. Something in Cleo melted, she could not be angry with the child because she was innocent. She even found it hard to be upset with the young woman because she was young and foolish. But, she was seething inside knowing that Michael had betrayed her.

"Look Paula, Michael is not doing very well. I can't let you see him because I'm afraid the shock of him knowing I know about the child and the affair may set him back and impede his healing. Just let me have your phone number and address and I promise to call you tomorrow to work something out about the child support payments. When Michael is stronger, the three of us can then talk about the child and go from there."

After Paula left, Cleopatra finished Michael's lunch and numbly walked up the stairs with the tray in her hand. Her mind was spinning in several directions and a feeling a betrayal was invading her very being. How could he have done this to her? Having a child with another woman was bad enough, but her having to find out about the affair from the other woman, who had the nerve to bring his illegitimate daughter into her home, was too much. She wouldn't jeopardize Michael's health by confronting him now but in time there would have to be a meeting of the minds and decisions made about their marriage.

Mercedes M. Alexander

Michael smiled when he saw Cleo enter the bedroom. "Thanks honey, that smells real good." "Did I hear the door bell a little while ago?"

"Yes you did Michael, it was just somebody trying to sell vacuum cleaners."

* * *

The next morning Cleo called Michael's mother and asked if she would sit with him while she ran errands during the day. Jerry Beavers was more than happy to do so. She had been thinking that Cleo was spending too much time in the house with Michael and needed to get out and do things with her friends.

As soon as Cleopatra had gotten out of the driveway, she picked up her cell phone and called the number Paula had given her.

"Hello, Paula? This is Cleopatra Beavers, I wanted to come by and talk with you and your grandmother this morning if it's possible."

"That's fine, Mrs. Beavers. We'll be here and you can come at any time. My grandmother is anxious to meet you and I did tell her that you would be calling."

"Alright then, I'll see you within the hour."

Cleopatra clicked off the phone and immediately headed toward Pat's house. There were just some things a woman needed to talk to her girlfriend about and this was just one of those things. The fact that Cleopatra was now not feeling any anger toward anyone about the affair or the baby was odd. But she had rationalized during the night that she almost made the same mistake with Leonard Wilkins and she knew from experience just how easily affairs could start. However, she had made only

Cleopatra's New Attitude

one slip up during her marriage, now she was wondering how many other women her husband had fooled around with. Michael was too fragile to be put in the position of knowing that Cleopatra knew the whole sordid story. She did not want him upset and for some unknown reason, she had made the decision to wait until a later time to tell Michael she knew about Paula and Alexis.

*   *   *

"Hush your mouth Cleo, you know that cannot be true." Michael has always worshipped you and I just refuse to believe he had a baby with some young girl while carrying on an affair."

"It's true Pat, when I looked into that baby's eyes all I could see was Michael. She has his eyes, his nose and his dimples. If you were looking at his baby pictures and then looked at her, you would think it was the same child. She is the prettiest child I have ever seen and seems to be such a good baby. The mother has a quiet demeanor about herself and was clearly embarrassed about the situation."

"Well, hell, I would have been embarrassed too. Just what did she think she was doing walking up to your house with that little monkey on her hip and giving you some sob story about not getting her child support checks. I would have kicked the little whore to the curb."

"I couldn't do that Pat. Everybody makes mistakes and who am I to judge. I'm going to meet with her today and offer to give her the child support each month until Michael is better and we can work something else out."

Pat looked over at her friend and completely lost it. She could not believe what was coming out of Cleopatra's mouth. Had her friend snapped under the strain of taking care of Michael and then finding out about his affair?

"Cleo, don't go there. You need to take your time and think about this situation long and hard. I agree that it's not the time to tell Michael you know everything about his little fling, but in time you need to confront him. And, you don't know if that little grave digger ever received a child support check or just how much Michael gave her. You need to check that one out further before you hand over one red penny to the little crumb snatcher."

"I know Pat, but as I said before, now is not the time for any showdowns. I just want to take this slowly. After I talk with Paula and her grandmother today maybe my head will be a little clearer on just what I need to do. I did look through Michael's past bank statements while he was sleeping and it seems that exactly 17 months ago he started writing a $350 check each month to a Mrs. Elaine Williams. I assume she's the grandmother. I wonder just how many times Michael has seen the child and if he has any type of relationship as a parent with her. I guess I'll find out about all of that shortly, I need to get going and take care of the business at hand. Thanks for talking with me and don't tell Annette or Kathy about any of this, I will do that myself."

Pat gave her friend a long hug and promised to be there for her. She watched Cleo drive down the street and thought that her friend had too much on her plate to handle. As Pat walked back into her house her only thought was, *I would kill the son of a bitch, sick or no sick!*

Cleopatra's New Attitude

*   *   *

Cleo had no problem finding the house. It was located in a very poor section of town and although it was a small house with nothing distinctive about it, the yard was full of beautiful flowers and seemed to be well kept. Parking her car in the driveway, she looked around and saw children running and playing all around the neighborhood. It looked like a friendly street where a child could be safely raised. Getting out of the car, she noticed neighbors talking over fences to each other and older ladies out watering flowers. Her mind wandered to a place long ago when her grandmother was alive and lived in just such a neighborhood. She could remember the good times she had at "nana's" house and all the friends her grandmother had in her neighborhood. As she walked up to the front door, she suddenly realized how apprehensive she was about meeting the grandmother and seeing the child again. *Maybe this is a mistake. I really don't know what I'm walking into. I should just leave this alone and let Michael handle it when he gets back on his feet again.* Before Cleo could turn around, an older woman appeared in the doorway with a large smile on her face.

"Well hello there, now you must be Mrs. Beavers, I'm Elaine Williams, Lordy, Lordy my grandchild described you to a tee. Please, please come right on in and have a seat."

Cleo reluctantly walked through the door and took a seat in the nearest chair. The room was immaculate, there was nothing out of place and the furniture although old was very well kept. There was a pleasant smell in the air that reminded her of her grandmother's vanilla teacakes. As she took her seat, the little old lady started rattling on and on about how relieved she was that Cleo came to visit.

Mercedes M. Alexander

"I can't tell you how much I wanted to pick up that telephone and call you a number of times. When my granddaughter told me you were coming, I sent her to the store so that I could have a little time to talk with you alone."

Mrs. Williams was talking while fidgeting around with the little white dollies sitting on the edge of each arm of her chair. She seemed very fragile and a little nervous. Cleopatra's heart went out to the older woman. Here she was in her twilight years and trying to raise a small child. Mrs. Williams spoke again as if she had read Cleo's mind.

"As you can see, I'm a little old to be trying to raise a baby, but I had no choice. My granddaughter is not interested in being a parent and just left that little girl and went running off to another part of the country. She hardly ever calls and only sees the child every two or three months for a weekend. The only reason she came back this time was to find out why the support checks had stopped. When she got here, one of her friends told her about the coach's heart attack."

"Mrs. Williams, did Paula tell you that I knew nothing about the child?"

Paula's grandmother sat and stared at Cleopatra, she was having a little trouble comprehending Cleo's last statement.

"You mean to tell me your husband didn't tell you about Alexis! I was so sure that he had, he would come and personally bring the check to me and he just adores the child. He never forgets her during the holidays, took her shopping by himself on her birthday and calls her his little angel. I can't believe he never said anything to you. I am so sorry, I know this must be a shock."

Cleopatra's New Attitude

"Yes, Mrs. Williams, it was a shock and I haven't told my husband that I know about Paula and the baby. He is not responding to his medication as expected and I don't want to do or say anything right now to upset him. I will deal with him in my own time. However, I wanted to talk with you to see exactly what you need for the child. I know you have not received any type of support from Michael lately and I am willing to help you financially."

"Bless your heart baby, I sho' appreciate your generosity. But, I needed to talk to you about more than financial support. As I told you before Paula is not a good parent and I'm too old to be raising a child. I wanted to talk with you about you and your husband taking little Alexis and legally adopting her so she can have a home with a mother and a father."

The room began to spin and Cleo had to grab the end of the sofa to settle herself. Did she hear what she thought she heard? Mrs. Williams couldn't possibly want her to raise her husband's love child and what would Paula say. This was slowly becoming a very bad dream and she needed to wake up and soon.

The front door swung open and in stepped Paula with a young man in tow. She put her bags from the store on the dining room table and walked over to introduce her friend to Cleo and to her grandmother.

"Grandma, Mrs. Beavers, I want you to meet Tyrone, he's from Chicago. He was pulling in the driveway as I approached the house. I didn't know he was coming but it is a wonderful surprise. Tyrone and I are sort of living together."

The look on Paula's grandmother's face was one of displeasure. Apparently she did not know Paula was living with a man. Mrs. Williams had apparently raised her granddaughter in the church and shacking up with a man was not what a respectable young woman should be doing.

Mercedes M. Alexander

Seeing that the situation was getting strained, Cleo immediately extended her hand to greet Tyrone.

"Tyrone, what a nice masculine name, but I didn't get your last name."

"Sorry, Paula did not tell you my last name, it's Abernathy. It's very nice to meet you and you too Mrs. Williams. Paula has told me so much about her grandmother and how much you have done for her. She didn't know I was coming, I got a few days off from work and decided to drive down and surprise her."

Paula was a little nervous and moved around the room as if she was looking for something. She never asked Tyrone to take a seat and she kept looking toward the back of the house. Just as Cleo's eyes looked toward the hallway, little Alexis appeared rubbing her eyes. She had apparently been asleep and was stumbling toward her great-grandmother.

"There's my little angel," exclaimed Mrs. Williams. "Did you get finished with your nap sweetie? Look who's here."

The child looked at Cleopatra and smiled while holding tightly to her granny.

Tyrone Abernathy looked from Paula to Mrs. Williams to the baby. He had a look in his eye that gave Cleo immediate knowledge that Paula had not told her live-in lover she had a child. She could see the question of "who's child is that" on the tip of his tongue and she also saw a nervous Paula Mims breaking out in a sweat. The web of deceit was growing thicker by the minute and Cleopatra could see disaster looming in the immediate future.

"Paula, could you and Tyrone be kind enough to take Alexis outside while your grandmother and I finish discussing our business? I'll need her

Cleopatra's New Attitude

to keep the baby for me for a few more days while I take care of things for my job out of town."

Paula quickly swooped the child in her arms. "Sure Mrs. Beavers, I'll be more than happy to take her outside. Come on Tyrone, let's take her down the street to the park and let her swing on the kiddy swing for a while."

After Tyrone and Paula left, Mrs. Williams flopped down on the sofa with large tears falling from her eyes. "I just don't know what to do or who to turn to at this point Mrs. Beavers. You saw the look on Paula's face when she thought the cat was out of the bag. She's never told that boy about her baby and I suspect she doesn't intend to tell him. She's started a new life and a baby does not fit into the picture. Besides, I'm a little uneasy with her having strange men around my little angel. You read all the time about these men doing ugly things to little girls that do not belong to them. Lord have mercy, just what am I suppose to do."

Cleopatra looked at the older woman and knew just what she was talking about and what she was thinking. At the age of 80, Mrs. Williams probably did not have the stamina to raise an active 18 month old child and she could become ill at anytime. What would become of the child then?

"Mrs. Williams, please pull yourself together, there's a solution to every problem, we just have to take our time and try to find it. In the meantime, please take this check and I'll be in touch within the next few days."

As Cleo drove away from the house, she looked back and saw the elder woman standing in the doorway. Her heart went out to her and she wondered how Michael would respond to the fact that if anything happened to Mrs. Williams, his child could easily end up being a ward of the state of Tennessee.

CHAPTER 14

"Have you seen her? Tell me have you seen her . . . ."

Leonard Wilkins was keeping his mind occupied with his work. He had not socialized in months and had resigned himself to being alone and not needing the company of any woman for a long time to come. At this point in his life, if he could not have Cleopatra Beavers he would not waste his time with other women trying to fill the void. As far as he was concerned, there was not a woman anywhere that would compare to Cleo.

Keeping himself busy on the weekends and working hard during the week became his salvation. Leonard had found God and decided to dedicate his life to Christ. At one of the lowest points in his life, he started going to church regularly. The Rev. Byron Handy of Bethel Baptist Church had become his spiritual leader and asked him to work with the church's youth program on Saturdays. Leonard was hesitant at first about spending time with the youth group, what did he have to share and how would he relate to them? The very first Saturday spent with them revealed to Leonard that he had a chance to experience things now as a role model that he never had experienced while growing up. There was never a man

Mercedes M. Alexander

around to throw a baseball to him and during his high school years of playing football and basketball, he didn't have anyone to watch and tell him how proud they were of his accomplishments. Seeing the smiles on the faces of the little boys on his basketball team when he praised them did something for him, he was starting to feel like Rev. Handy said he would—a real man.

One of the six year olds by the name of Matthew Allen had become Leonard's favorite little sidekick on Saturdays. Matthew was not a very good basketball player and was small for his age but his eagerness to play and his enthusiasm made him Leonard's little hero. Matthew was being raised by elderly grandparents and never knew his mother or father. His mom died during childbirth and his father had always been unknown to the grandparents. His grandparents gave all they could to him but just didn't have the energy to keep up with an active six year old boy. They were more than happy when Leonard started showing special interest in Matthew and began to take him on various outings for the weekend.

Leonard would watch Matt and wonder just how it would be if he were his father. He knew from the way Matt would cling to him when it was time for him to go home that the little boy had developed a great affection for him. Leonard also knew that he had come to love the little boy and would do just about anything in the world for him. The willingness of the grandparents to share Matt with Leonard was the perfect solution, it helped to keep loneliness from knocking at Leonard's door. Leonard had now built a small world around his job, his church and Matthew.

Today Leonard took Matt to the mall for new tennis shoes. He watched as the little boy ran with excitement in and out of the stores. Leonard walked behind Matt with his hands in his pockets jingling the

Cleopatra's New Attitude

change in them. It was amazing how much energy the little chap had, Leonard was worn out just following behind him at a rapid pace. It was time for lunch and the food court was just around the corner. Catching up with Matthew, Leonard grabbed his hand and pulled him in the direction of something that was smelling mighty good. The offer of food always got Matt's attention and he was sure to ask for nothing more than a hamburger and French fries.

Being an inquisitive little boy, Matt asked Leonard all types of questions. Leonard answered them as best he could, but nine times out of ten if Matt asked the question, he already knew the answer. As they sat and ate, the look on the child's face was a warning that he was ready to bombard his mentor with questions.

"Mister Leonard, how come you don't have a wife? Mr. Leonard, who's gonna cook for you when you get old? Mr. Leonard, do you have a girlfriend?"

"Ok Matt, slow your roll and stop worrying about me needing a wife or a girlfriend," chuckled Leonard. *Goodness the child never lets his mouth rest and you can't get angry with him because every question is asked with that silly grin on his face.* "Let's concentrate on buying some tennis shoes today. The ones you've been wearing are old and you need a little pep in your step. You know—if we buy some of those Michael Jordan tennis shoes I bet you could jump as high as he can!"

"Aw Mister Leonard, I'm too little to jump that high but when I grow up, I'm gonna knock that ball in the hoop so hard it'll break the glass like some of the pros do."

Leonard laughed at the little smurf with the big ideas. *Oh, to be a child again and think that everything is right with the world.*

Mercedes M. Alexander

After lunch and going through the ritual of trying on twenty pairs of tennis shoes before a decision was made by Matthew, the two of them headed toward home. As Leonard took the little boy to the front door of his grandparent's house he was immediately stricken with the feeling that he did not want to deposit his little buddy back home so soon. Matthew did not want to go home either, but was promised by Leonard that they would do something special the next weekend.

On the ride home, Leonard made a detour just to drive by Cleo's house. He knew of Michael's illness and worried about how Cleopatra was handling the stress of caring for her sick husband. After hiring a private investigator to keep an eye on Cleopatra and give him the low down on Michael, Leonard was told about Mike's indiscretions and his love child. His first inclination was to present Cleopatra with his findings but he knew that confronting her would only make her push him away even more. How could he have justified hiring a private investigator to snoop in her husband's affairs? Even if he did have the goods on Michael, presenting them to Cleo was another matter. He knew in his heart that Michael was not the man for Cleo and vowed to watch and wait until his time came to claim her for himself.

While slowly cruising down the street he saw just what he wanted. Cleopatra was unloading bags from her car with the help of one of the neighborhood boys. Leonard pulled over to the opposite side of the street and just sat and watched her. Lord, what he wouldn't do to have her in his life. He was mesmerized by her movements and noticed that she seemed tired and was not her usual animated self.

As Leonard was sitting across the street watching Cleo's every move a familiar car drove up in her driveway. When the man got out, Leonard

Cleopatra's New Attitude

realized it was Rev. Handy and his wife. They both embraced Cleopatra and started helping with the bags by carrying the last of them into the house.

Well, life is full of surprises, thought Leonard. *I wonder how Rev. and Mrs. Handy know Cleopatra. She's not a member of our church and I've never seen her or Michael there. Maybe they are all just friends and the good Rev. Handy is making a visit to the sick. Whatever the reason this is interesting.*

CHAPTER 15

"Shake me, wake me when it's over . . . ."

Rachel Bennett had been one of Leonard's neighbors for years. She considered herself a friend to his ex-wife and was constantly in and out of their home. Although she had small features and was a five on a scale of 1 to 10, she was what the Black community would call high yellow and thought that was all she needed to get a man.

Rachel was one of the main people who told the ex-Mrs. Wilkins not to put up with Leonard's tricks. "Girl, if he was my husband, I would kick his ass to the curb. You're still young and can get another man. Don't waste your time with that wannabe pimp daddy."

Thinking her friend was her friend, Melissa took heed to her advice and left Leonard. Little did she know that Rachel was plotting all the time knowing that if Melissa actually left, she would return home to Mississippi and leave Leonard just where Rachel wanted him—alone and lonely. Rachel knew about his womanizing and could have cared less. All she wanted was the status of being Mrs. Leonard Wilkins and living in the lap of luxury—if she had to share him to get him, then so be it.

Mercedes M. Alexander

Always dropping in and out of Leonard's home, wanting to act as hostess for him when he had clients over for drinks and cooking elaborate meals for him were some of the tactics she used to worm her way into his life. She lost weight, changed her hairstyle, and bought a snazzy wardrobe, all to make Leonard notice her.

Leonard did notice, but was in the using mode when it came to her. He enjoyed her cooking and was glad to have a woman around when he entertained who would make drinks, serve whatever food was necessary and leave his house and kitchen spotless when everything ended. There was one thing Leonard noticed that was not to his liking, Rachel was starting to break down, Mother Nature was not being kind to her as she aged!

"Hello, Leonard, I thought I saw your car pass my house a minute ago and figured you were headed home. How was your day?"

"I've had a good day Rachel, I spent most of it mentoring for the church and really enjoyed myself."

"That's good Leonard," Rachel purred into the phone. "It's still very early and I was wondering if you've had dinner. If you're free and feel up to it, I have two tickets to a movie that premiers tonight and I'll treat you to a late dinner afterward."

"Thanks for the offer, but I've already decided to chill for the evening and maybe watch something on HBO. I'm just going to warm some Chinese leftovers I have in the fridge and call it a night."

Rachel was not about to take any form of rejection from Leonard tonight, she had plans for the man and was going to follow through with them no matter what.

Cleopatra's New Attitude

"Well, I just didn't want to spend the evening alone and wanted some company. Do you have enough leftovers for two? If you do, I would love to share them and watch whatever movie you want. Just let me come over and keep you company."

Not wanting to hurt Rachel's feelings, Leonard agreed to let her come. Little did he know that she purposefully dressed in a pair of spandex pants with a large baggy t-shirt and no underwear. She had decided that tonight was the night and what she had to lay on poor unsuspecting Leonard was something most men could not and would not turn down.

Rachel arrived grinning from ear to ear, knowing that getting her foot in the door this night would help her move her program along. Leonard Wilkins would be hers no matter what and she had learned long ago to be a patient woman. Things had been hard for Rachel in the last five years, a nasty divorce, failed romances and financial problems kept her wishing for brighter days. In the past when money was tight and she needed a little extra to get by on, Leonard had gladly helped his friend. Every time Leonard reached into his wallet to help her, Rachel believed that he was doing it not just out of friendship but maybe for something just a little more. To her, just a little more meant interest on Leonard's part in her well being which added up to interest in her personal life which added up to a possible romance. It was amazing how the woman could put two and two together and come up with five. In her mind, Leonard was very interested in her and only needed a little push from her to realize it. She would try everything in the book to give him that push, even to the point of being brazen with it.

"Well good evening Leonard," exclaimed Rachel as she entered the house.

Leonard noticed her obvious dress and the tone in her voice, which was a sexy whisper. He immediately knew this was going to be an interesting evening and that Rachel was making herself available.

"Hi Rachel, I see you've dressed comfortably and didn't waste any time coming over. Let's get my leftovers warmed and ready ourselves for the movie. I'm starved and want to get settled in and be able to prop my feet up to relax."

"No sooner said than done Leonard. You go into the den and get comfortable and I'll warm the food and bring it out to you." Rachel had a mischievous smile on her face and moved in so close to Leonard, he could smell the breath freshener she had obviously just used.

"If you insist, I'll take my leave and let you have the run of the kitchen."

Rachel pushed him toward the den and went straight into the kitchen, one that she knew very well. It didn't matter to her that there were five or six other women who knew his kitchen and his bed well enough to think they would one day be Mrs. Wilkins. She was here now and here she planned to stay. Moving efficiently in the kitchen and putting the food on a serving tray, Rachel happily moved toward the den with a greedy smile on her face. Tonight was the night!

CHAPTER 16

"Still Waters Run Deep . . . ."

Sunday morning came with a blast of sunlight in Leonard's face as he lay in bed. He was not feeling good about himself because he had done the nasty with Rachel during the night. He knew she was forcing herself on him but after three glasses of wine (which she conveniently brought with her) he was not in any condition to turn her down. Three glasses of wine will make a man not notice sagging breast and stretch marks. All he knew was there was something between a willing woman's legs that was calling his name ever so seductively. They just had sex with no feelings, no love shared, just raw sex. Afterward, Leonard couldn't look the woman in the face. He had used her for release of sexual tension, nothing more. As he closed his eyes during their sexual encounter, all he could see was Cleopatra's enticing smile and sexy body. He was making love to Cleopatra and Rachel was being used. Now he was just relieved she was gone, leaving him to chastise himself for falling into her planned trap—one he knew she was planning the minute she walked through the door. Rachel slid out of Leonard's bed around midnight and went home with a large smile on her face. In her mind, this was just the beginning of more things to come.

Mercedes M. Alexander

Leonard looked over to the clock and realized if he did not hurry he would be late for 11 o'clock services at the church. He wanted to make sure he was in church today so that he could talk with the pastor after the services. Seeing Pastor Handy today was at the top of his list, he intended to worm his way into asking how the Reverend and his wife knew Cleopatra.

After the services, while everyone did their usual shaking of hands and small talk, Leonard purposefully made himself the last person to greet Rev. Handy.

"I really enjoyed your sermon today Pastor Handy. It seems that most of it was aimed directly at me, I had to stop and check myself a few times."

"Naw son, on any given day one of my sermons will hit most of my parishioners between the eyes. You see, we all sin in one form or another and we all could use a little forgiveness from time to time."

"Well pastor, I've found since I started really reading my bible that I need to ask for forgiveness from people I have known during my life. You see I always did what was best for Leonard and thought to hell with everybody else. Now that I have been saved, I know I need to make amends for my wrongdoings but I don't know how to go about doing that. Do you have any suggestions?"

"Well brother Leonard, asking for forgiveness from man is a good thing but first you need to seek forgiveness from the Lord. Then and only then will you be set free and everything else will fall into place."

"I understand that and I know God will forgive me, but people are very slow to forgive because they refuse to forget what happened in the past."

Cleopatra's New Attitude

Pastor Handy could see that Leonard was really troubled and decided to invite him to Sunday dinner so they could finish their discussion. Leonard quickly jumped at the invitation.

*   *   *

Mrs. Handy could really throw down in the kitchen. Leonard could not remember the last time he had such good down home cooking. After the meal, he offered to help with the dishes but Mrs. Handy refused to let him come near the kitchen. She insisted he go into the den with Pastor Handy and relax. Although Leonard tried to push the point that he knew his way around a kitchen and he really wanted to help her with the dishes, she gently shoved him toward the door of the den.

"Son, you might as well let her have her kitchen to herself," exclaimed Pastor Handy. "She considers that place her private domain and I enter only when the queen demands my presence."

Mrs. Handy gave the Reverend a loving peck on his cheek and a knowing smile. "Keep talking old man, not only am I the queen of this kitchen, I'm the empress of this house and I want the two of you out of my way. Now scat!"

Laughing at her comments the two men took their leave and headed toward the family den. Both of them were grateful their presence in the kitchen was not wanted. Reverend Handy did want to talk to Leonard about his work in the church and his last conversation with Matthew Allen's grandparents. Leonard had his own personal agenda, he wanted to pump the Reverend for information about his knowledge of Cleopatra Beavers.

Mercedes M. Alexander

When Leonard took his seat in the den, his eyes wandered along the walls of the big room. He was taken back and marveled at how tastefully decorated the room was. It was a man's room with large furniture, a game table and a huge big screen television that was immediately turned on with the old preacher flipping channels looking for the featured Sunday football game. While getting acquainted with the room, Leonard's eyes fell upon a group of pictures on the mantel of the fireplace. The very first picture he noticed was one of Cleopatra dressed in a cap and gown!

"Well brother Leonard, I hope you enjoyed the sermon today. I really had a hard time this week trying to understand just what the Lord wanted me to preach about but something interesting happened last Friday night at my meeting with the deacons and trustees of the church, and I knew exactly what the sermon needed to be for today."

"I thought your subject of "Dry Bones" was intriguing. It never ceases to amaze me how your sermons seem to make me squirm along with the other members of the church thinking you're preaching directly at me. However, from my seat in the front side pew I did notice a few of your deacons on the front with huge frowns on their faces."

"Disgust on their faces would more accurately describe it," chuckled Pastor Handy. Between three of them sitting there sleep throughout the entire sermon and the other seven trying to stare me down, I don't think I reached a one of them."

"Well, just why did you preach about dry bones? I mean, I know what the gist of the sermon was about, it seems that some of your leaders have a problem with faith and vision. I'm not up on my bible like I should be, but I do know that Ezekiel preached to the dry bones because God commanded him to do so."

Cleopatra's New Attitude

Reverend Handy walked to the fireplace and placed his hands on the mantel. He seemed deep in thought and turned quietly to face Leonard.

"Ezekiel was a priest and a prophet in the old testament of the Bible," stated Pastor Handy. He ministered to his people during the darkest days of Judah's history when they were in Babylonian captivity. God wanted them to know that he was the Lord, so he took a valley of dry bones and made them into an army so his people would know he was God and nothing was impossible if only they put their trust in him. Well Leonard, our church is full of people without vision and we have a lot of unbelievers as to just what God can do sitting in the pews. I prayed that God would touch me today and breathe some life into those dry bones in our church."

"I think you did Reverend, a few of the sisters tried to break down their own personal pews with their shouting today and Sister Earnestean needs to be sent a bill for the wall she tore down."

Both of the men roared and talked more about what needed to change in the church and positions that needed to be created so that the church would continue to grow and do more things to involve the membership and the community. Rev. Handy was becoming very attached to Leonard. He saw in him a great potential to become a leader in his church. Even though he knew about Leonard's so called sordid past, he knew that salvation could make him a work of art designed exclusively by God for all men to see. A number of the women in the church had come to him with their gossip about what they had heard in the community concerning Leonard's lifestyle. Some of them went as far as telling Rev. Handy that Leonard would be a distraction in the church and would corrupt some of the younger women. They also told him they feared some of the young men would imitate Leonard through hero worship and would fall from

Mercedes M. Alexander

grace by following a man with such a despicable history. Pastor Handy only chastised them for judging and quickly quoted scriptures about how God used some of the most sinful characters in the Bible to reach his people. Needless to say, some of the women refused to back off and would continue to rip Leonard up one wall and down another with Pastor Handy always defending him. The seasoned Preacher also knew that some of the same women complaining to him had past lives that would make Leonard look like a saint. He had decided long ago that he had members who were so heavenly bound they were no earthly good. He always knew God put these people in his path to keep him grounded.

"Leonard, I've been wanting to talk to you for a few weeks now about your relationship with Matthew. I have noticed how much time you spend with the boy and his grandparents think you have been a blessing to him. The grandparents are up in age now and Mr. Allen has just been diagnosed with a heart conditioned. Mrs. Allen has been ill with diabetes for years and the two of them just can't continue to raise little Matthew. They approached me and wanted my input on their thoughts about asking you to be Matthew's legal guardian."

Floored by the Pastor's statement, Leonard sat in the comfortable recliner and just stared at the preacher. Never in his wildest dreams did he think he would be having a conversation with anyone about him becoming a single parent. The thought was overwhelming and although frightening, gave Leonard a little tingle of joy. He knew Matthew was in need of someone to really look after him and there seemed to have been a connection between the two of them from the instant they started hanging together. However, he still had doubts about parenting and being totally responsible for raising a young boy. Was he really cut-out for this?

"Well, this comes as a shocker! I enjoy being with Matthew and I know the situation at the Allen's home. Just how did this conversation come up Reverend and why do they think I would be a good parent to the child?"

The old preacher stood up again and walked to the window. Taking his time before answering Leonard's question and staring up toward the sky making Leonard feel a little uneasy. There was something almost ethereal about the moment, the preacher felt it and so did Leonard.

"Son, I don't know why but there's something about you that makes me know without a doubt that you can do this and there are better things ahead for you. You need to pray about this and trust that God knows what he's doing."

Sitting in almost a stupor, Leonard instantly knew he had to take responsibility for Matthew. He could not put his finger on it, but he felt there was a reason for this situation and that his life was about to change for the better. Smiling at the preacher and shaking his head, Leonard forgot to ask about the picture on the mantel.

CHAPTER 17

"Bridge over troubled water . . . ."

Pat Jackson was not a woman to sit on her bottom and watch her friend suffer at the hands of a man who had betrayed her. Small in stature but big in attitude, Pat was outraged about the entire situation. How dare the man do such a thing to Cleo and here he was now flat on his back dependent upon her to take care of him. Divorced twice, Pat knew the ins and outs of how men displayed their infidelity and the price women paid for loving these men. Michael Beavers was not about to get away with this one, he had committed the crime of the century as far as she was concerned and he deserved no sympathy from any woman. She hoped that while he was lying flat on his back and almost totally helpless, his life would flash across his mind and make him feel ashamed of himself. Although she had promised Cleopatra that she would not tell anyone about Michael's love child, she decided some action needed to be taken and so she called a meeting of the Golden Girls—minus Cleopatra.

"Alright Pat, you know I rip and run every Saturday morning trying to shop and do house work. This emergency call meeting had better be good," sighed Annette.

Mercedes M. Alexander

Kathy was moving in a daze as if 8 am in the morning was a curse. She looked as if she had been out half the night and needed at least another four hours of sleep. Moving slowly to the coffee pot and not looking at anybody in particular she turned and reached for the croissants while pouring coffee.

"Looks to me as if this meeting is about Cleo since she's the only one not here," stated Kathy as she sipped her coffee.

"Yes this meeting is about her and hurry and sit your dizzy behind down so we can get started," Pat said as she pushed the girl toward the table. "I know you two have things to do this morning but Cleo is in trouble and we need to put our heads together and talk about her situation before we discuss anything with her present."

"What do you mean by she's in trouble?" questioned Annette while stirring her coffee. "We know about her troubles with the infamous Leonard Wilkins and as far as I'm concern we need to finalize our plans about his final punishment at the hands of the Golden Girls."

"We'll have to put Leonard Wilkins on the back burner for now. He's not the most important issue at hand right now. Cleopatra has bigger problems than the one she had with the little gigolo." Putting the coffee pot in the center of the table on a hot plate, Pat pulled a chair out. "She has problems that I'm afraid she can't handle and I seriously think she might be losing it."

Pat sat down at the kitchen table and told her buddies about the new developments in Cleopatra's life. She took her time and told the entire sordid story of Michael's indiscretions, the baby born during his affair and the fact that he had been paying child support and never told Cleopatra. She also informed them that while snooping around she had been told by several other women that they knew about the baby and Michael had had affairs with at least two other much younger women. Her biggest concern now was that Cleopatra did not know about the other women.

In total shock over the newest revelations, Annette and Kathy sat with their mouths open. Nobody said a word for several minutes and the silence in the room was deafening.

Kathy was the first to speak. "I think I'm going to be sick. How could Michael do such a thing to Cleopatra. He knew how devastated she was about not being able to have children and then the low life bastard goes out and has a baby by a younger woman and someone who was a student of his at that. He was probably smart enough to wait just long enough until they all were of legal age before he made his move, now he's labeled a pervert in my book. The ironic part of this whole thing is that Cleo was mentally punishing herself for her innocent friendship with Leonard Wilkins and one silly kiss while her husband was screwing every young thing willing to open her legs to him."

"I'm afraid ladies there is nothing we can do about this one. We will just have to let her know that we will be there for her when she needs us. I'm not one to give advice to a woman about her husband. I know from experience if I tell a woman how big of an asshole her husband is and then they make up and stay together, I'm the one left feeling like a fool and probably a fool with one less friend because I opened my big mouth. I don't truly believe that would be the case with Cleo, but I don't want to take the chance." After making this statement, Annette stood to leave.

"Just wait a damn minute," yelled Pat. "I didn't call you two over to get any negative feedback. I called you over here to tell you about Cleo's plight and to give you two heads up on her situation so that when you

Mercedes M. Alexander

hear it, it won't be a complete surprise. I know we can't do anything at this point but I do know that our friend will need us sooner than she thinks once she finds out about the other women. Now I promised her I wouldn't tell either of you anything but this scenario started as a small snowball and it's growing by the day. I think she's in denial right now because the girl actually went over to the baby's grandmother's house and paid child support for the last few months missed by Michael. She hasn't told him she knows about the baby and says she's waiting for him to get better before she does. The real sick part is that she talked about how cute the child was and how innocent the mother looked. When she finds out about the other women she'll probably freak out and need us."

The three women agreed they would watch and see what happened with Cleo's situation. They were all determined to be there for her when they were needed but neither of them would tell her about the other women.

After Annette and Kathy left, Pat decided to call Cleopatra and check on her. She had not talked to her since she stopped by a few days ago to drop the bomb about Michael's baby.

"Hey girlfriend, it's me. I'm just calling to check on you and see if you needed anything while I'm out today. I know you're basically tied to the house and I don't mind doing your shopping for you today. If you need me to, I can come by and help with the cleaning."

Cleopatra was touched, this was truly her friend and right now she needed just to talk and forget about what was going on in her household.

"Thanks Pat, I had a chance to go shopping yesterday and the house is clean. Being at home all the time gives me plenty of opportunity to keep

Cleopatra's New Attitude

my home in good order. I don't think it's been this clean since I moved in here years ago,"

"Well, if you don't mind, I'll drop by this afternoon just to look in on you and see for myself that you're alright. I baked one of those 7-Up cakes you like last night and I'll bring some of it with me. We can sit and have coffee with the cake and catch up on our church gossip."

"That would be great, I would love to have the company. I'll be here all day so drop in whenever you want."

"OK, see you in a few girlfriend."

As Cleopatra put the receiver back into the cradle of the phone she knew something was bothering Pat. Bringing cake over was just an excuse to get her foot in the door. The last thing she wanted was pity from Pat about her situation with Michael, but she also knew Pat would be there for her come hell or high water because she was just that kind of friend.

CHAPTER 18

"RESPECT, find out what it means to me . . . ."

Rushing around the house trying to get her morning work done and finishing breakfast for Michael, Cleopatra was already tired and wanting to rest before 10 o'clock. Her Saturdays were once her lazy days when she could leisurely shop in the malls during the day and do a quick grocery store check before she returned home. Now she spent her Saturdays cooking and cleaning.

Michael, although not helpless, had turned to a mama's baby and wanted Cleo around all the time. He spent most of his time upstairs sitting around in the recliner Cleo had purchased for him so that he would not lie in bed while watching the television. He was gaining his weight back and his energy was building daily. A few of his buddies would drop by the house from time to time and offer to sit with him and let Cleo have some time to herself. During one of these times Michael's friend, Reggie, gave him the heads up on what he had seen while visiting his children on the other side of town. He had seen Cleo standing outside Elaine William's house holding a small child and talking with the older woman. This was

Mercedes M. Alexander

an area of town where Reggie's ex-wife and children lived and according to his children, Cleo had been seen there twice visiting the old woman.

Michael had immediately panicked, Cleopatra now knew about the child and Paula. If she knew about them, it would only be a matter of time before she found out about the others and his marriage would be doomed. He had realized long ago just how much he loved Cleo and now the thought of losing her was crushing. He lied to his friend and pretended to need sleep so that Reggie would leave. Now he was just waiting for the bomb to drop.

*   *   *

Clearing the kitchen and waiting for Pat to arrive, Cleo began to prepare for her Sunday dinner. She had decided to invite both sets of parents over and maybe talk them into spending most of the evening to play a family game of Monopoly. It had been quite a while since she had entertained anyone and a little fun and games with family was something she thought would cheer Michael up and give all of them time to talk and visit.

The doorbell rang just as Cleo finished her potato salad for Sunday. Placing the dish in the refrigerator, she rushed to the door knowing it was Pat. As she opened the door and greeted her friend, she noticed Annette's car pulling up behind Pat's car.

"My, my, why am I the popular one today! First you call wanting to come and visit and now Annette is pulling up in the driveway directly behind you."

Pat jerked her head around to see Annette getting out of her vehicle and heading toward the door with a look of determination on her face.

Cleopatra's New Attitude

She immediately sensed trouble because Annette was walking fast and mumbling to herself. *Oh God*, she thought, *she's going to blab everything.*

As Annette entered the door, she immediately grabbed Cleopatra and hugged her. Caught off guard, Cleo had to balance herself because Annette had put a grip on her that jarred her from her stance. Cleo also noticed her cheek was wet and realized Annette was crying!

"Step back Pat," Annette commanded as she pushed her to the side. "I know what we discussed this morning and I know I said I was going to stay out of this, but while driving around I realized that as a friend to Cleo, I had to tell her this for her own good."

Cleo looked from one of her girlfriends to the other, what was going on and why was Pat looking at Annette as if she could stab her.

"Alright sisters, take a seat and tell me what is so damn important that one of you is crying and the other has the look of "I'm going to kill you" on her face." Looking at Pat, now staring at the floor, and then looking at Annette, huffing and puffing as if she wanted to fight, Cleopatra thought maybe something had occurred between the two women and she would have to be the referee.

Pat spoke first. "Well I guess we have to get this done and over with. Cleopatra, I know I promised not to tell Annette and Kathy about Michael's baby and young hoochie, but I thought they needed to know so that we could do our best to be there for you."

Shaking her head and looking at Pat with a knowing smile, Cleopatra wasn't angry about the betrayal.

"Girl, I knew you couldn't keep that information to yourself and I also knew you would only tell Annette and Kathy. This saves me from having to repeat the sordid tale. I'm not mad at you about that and thanks for confessing." Looking over to Annette, Cleo replied, "don't be so huffy about the situation Annette, I will handle this in my own way and I'll be just fine."

"No you won't be just fine Cleo, Pat has not told you the entire story. Our conversation was more than just about the baby and girlfriend. It was about the baby, the girlfriend and all the other girlfriends."

Slowly taking her seat, Cleopatra was not believing what she had just heard. Did Annette say "and all the other girlfriends" or was she hearing things?"

Rushing to her side Pat took her friend's hand. "Regardless to what people are saying and what Michael has been doing this is something you have to handle yourself. Whatever decision you make I want you to know that we'll stand with you and give all the support we can."

"Just what are people saying and how many other girlfriends are you talking about? Tell me now and stop trying to shield me from anything, I need to know so I can truthfully deal with this."

Pat and Annette told the entire story to Cleo and sat waiting for her to explode. Instead, Cleopatra walked to the kitchen and began pouring coffee for her friends and changed the conversation to what she had planned for Sunday evening. Her friends thought she was shutting down and going into complete denial. Little did they know that Cleo was now plotting her path of revenge against a man she thought loved her and had betrayed her in the worst way possible.

Entering the living room with a tray of coffee and slices of the 7-up cake Pat had provided, Cleo assured her friends she would be fine and that she needed to handle this in her own way. Her calmness was unnerving to Pat and Annette, it was not natural for a woman to hear such things about

Cleopatra's New Attitude

her husband and not start yelling and crying about how betrayed she felt and how she would repay the bastard.

After sitting and talking for another half hour, Cleo told her friends she had some errands to run and needed to get herself together. Pat and Annette reluctantly left and made Cleo promise to call if she needed to talk. Pat's first inclination was to gather all the knives in the house and take them with her. She later decided that death by stabbing was too good for Michael and believed that Cleopatra would make him suffer in her own quiet way.

Looking out the doorway and waving to her friends as they left the driveway, Cleopatra felt as if the world had been placed on her shoulders. She also remembered she had failed to tell her friends that little Miss Paula was a white girl and wondered just what the racial background of all the other women were. Michael was probably one of those equal opportunity lovers, race did not matter, they only had to meet one requirement to qualify for the job, a vagina and whorish ways. She had pledged while on the cruise to be a good wife to Michael and love him according to their vows "till death do us part." Now she was plundering whether the "till death do us part" should be by her own hand or should she wait for the hand of God to smite the low-down son-of-a-bitch.

* * *

After church, Cleopatra hurried about the kitchen to make sure everything was just right for her small dinner party. Her parents and Michael's parents would be arriving within the hour and she rushed around trying to put the final touches on the dining room table.

115

Mercedes M. Alexander

At exactly 3 o'clock the doorbell rang, John and Jerry Beavers were right on time. Cleo knew her parents would probably be running a few minutes late. It was hard for a minister to get away from members of his congregation on Sundays and there were always one or two of his members standing and waiting to have words with the Pastor after every sermon.

"Come on in, you're on time and what is that you're carrying that smells so good Jerry? Don't tell me it's one of your famous strawberry cakes!"

"Yes honey it is, I know you and Michael love strawberry cake and I decided to surprise you two with one today."

Cleo smiled at the couple and ushered them into the living room. She wondered if they knew what a bastard they had raised and if Michael had ever shared any of his nasty little secrets with his father. Cleo had heard through the grapevine about John Beavers and his dallying around town in his younger days with other women. The old saying of "chip off the old block" was fitting for Michael and John Beavers. She also wondered how Jerry could have stayed with him and how she handled the situation. Surely, she did not have to deal with an outside child and the fact that her husband was taking money out of the family finances because he had to pay child support.

Exactly fifteen minutes later, the Handy's arrived carrying a beautiful bouquet of tiger lilies. They apologized for being late and started right in wanting to know what was happening in the lives of John and Jerry since they had not seen them in some time. As the older adults sat and talked, Cleopatra ran upstairs to tell Michael that everyone had arrive and he should come down so they could get their dinner started. Michael reached for his wife and gave her a warm and tender kiss on her mouth.

Cleopatra's New Attitude

"Thanks honey for inviting the family over. My folks love to visit with your parents and this will give all of us time to talk and catch up on each other's lives."

Little did Michael know, this would be the last kiss he would ever plant on her lips and his parents would be seeing a lot more of him, especially since she was putting him out of her home today.

CHAPTER 19

"Ooo, Baby, Baby . . . ."

Cleopatra was the perfect hostess during the dinner. Everybody seemed to be enjoying themselves and the meal was delicious. Both sets of parents told Cleopatra and Michael how proud they were of them and the Beavers' praised Cleo and told her how thankful they were to her for nursing Michael back to health. It seemed to be a wonderful evening and Michael was beaming with pride as Cleo excused herself and told everyone that she would serve dessert with coffee in the living room.

"Tell us just how you're really feeling Michael?" asked Mrs. Handy. "You look like the picture of health to us now, but looks can be deceiving."

"I feel good Mother Beavers, Cleo has been the best nurse and my doctors are now pleased with my progress and said I could return to work in the fall. I've been told that after I fully recuperate I will feel better than I have in years."

Entering the room with a tray of steaming coffee and strawberry cake, Cleopatra set the tray right in front of Michael. She then walked across the room and leaned against the piano while staring directly at him.

"Go ahead and serve yourself first Michael, I'm sure you feel you deserve to have your cake and eat it too as the old saying goes."

Thinking Cleopatra was joking, Michael reached for the cake and chuckled. "Why thanks honey, every man should have a wife like you."

"Don't you mean a "dumb wife" like me Michael, one who lives in the dark and doesn't know what's going on right under her nose."

Everyone in the room turned to look at Cleopatra. Not knowing why Cleo made her last statement, Mrs. Handy quickly cut in and asked why was she standing on the other side of the room and whatever would make her say such a thing.

"Well Mother, apparently I have been the little dumb wife. I think I'll let Michael tell you just how dumb I've been while he's been making babies with other women all over town."

Everyone in the room then turned to look at Michael. Reverend Handy was the first to speak. "Maybe we all need to leave so that the two of you can talk. Get your things Della so we can take our leave."

"Hold on a minute daddy, nobody's going any damn where until "Mr. Ants In His Pants" tells you about his baby and all the other women in town he's been screwing."

Michael nervously put his coffee cup on the table and stood to his feet. "Your father's right Cleopatra. We need to talk privately."

"There will be no private talks in this house, people all over town are talking about you and your women so this situation is no longer a private one. Since the cat seems to have your tongue I guess I'll have to inform our parents just what kind of man you have proven to be."

Cleopatra took a seat opposite Michael and began telling about Paula and the baby. She described the day Paula showed up on her doorstep

Cleopatra's New Attitude

with the child and told of her meeting with Mrs. Williams. Mrs. Beavers was starting to look faint and Mr. Beavers got up and walked to the window. Nobody said a word and Cleopatra went on and on telling about Michael's indiscretions. She never realized that tears were streaming down her face and that her voice was getting shriller each second. By the time she finished telling her story she was screaming at Michael.

Michael walked over to Cleopatra and kneeled beside her chair. He reached to take her hand but thought better of doing that after he saw the look of "kill" on her face.

"Cleopatra, I can't tell you how sorry I am about what I've done. While lying flat on my back these last few months I have had my life flash by me over and over again and I have no excuse for what I did. I beg for your forgiveness and want you to let me make this up to you. I'll never violate our marriage again and promise to make you happy if you will give me another chance."

"I don't want you begging Michael, I want the complete truth and I want our parents to hear it from you right here and right now. Don't lie to us and remember that I know more than you think I know. Don't make me have to fill in any of the blanks in case you conveniently leave something out."

Looking like a beaten man, Michael started telling about his first affair with a woman he met who was the mother of one of his players. There were three other women before he started his affair with Paula. According to Michael, he had learned his lesson when Paula came up pregnant and instead of having an abortion as he had requested, she took his money and left town only to return with a baby in tow and wanting child support. Looking directly at Cleo, Michael begged again for her forgiveness he continued to tell her that he had wanted to confess to her about the child a number of times but never thought his timing was right. He swore he had nothing more to do with Paula but wanted to be a man and take care of his child financially. He even confessed to visiting the child frequently and taking her on outings to give Mrs. Williams some free time.

During the entire conversation between Cleopatra and Michael, neither of the parents said a word. They all looked stunned and were embarrassed to have to witness the disclosing of Michael's exploits.

Suddenly Jerry Beavers stood to her feet and walked over to Cleopatra. Putting her hand on Cleo's back she started patting her while a low moan started in the back of her throat and built to a deafening scream. She couldn't stop herself from crying and was totally out of control. Della Handy ran to her side and held her while Cleopatra stood to help her mother. Suddenly all the crying stopped and Mrs. Beavers pointed a finger at her husband.

"Well John, see how your son has followed in your footsteps. See how you have ruined his life by being less of a man and gloating to him about your women in the past. I should have put your low-life ass out years ago and maybe my child would not have used you as an example of what a man should be. You ought to be ashamed of yourself because the trouble brewing between Cleopatra and Michael now is because of the example you set for your son."

Grabbing her purse, Jerry Beavers asked Reverend and Mrs. Handy to please take her home. She then turned to Cleopatra and asked her to forgive her for not being a strong woman years ago and putting her husband out.

Cleopatra's New Attitude

"Before you leave Mother Beavers, please know that I don't blame you for any of this. Michael is a grown man and he made choices that put him in this position. Mr. Beavers, I want you to know that I hold no ill feelings toward you because you didn't do anything to me, your son did. However, when you leave I want the two of you to take Michael with you because he can't stay in this house another night."

After Cleopatra's statement all hell broke loose. Michael was ranting and raving that he wasn't about to leave his house. Rev. Handy was yelling that he would not let Michael disrespect his daughter and that he would be leaving that house and would leave it tonight. Mr. Beavers was denying that he had any influence over Michael and that his past affairs were long ago and his wife should not have been bringing up his past trying to make excuses for Michael. Mrs. Handy was trying to console her daughter by telling her that she did not have to put up with Michael and should put him out. And, Cleopatra was taking in the whole scene and wondering if all of them had lost their minds.

After all the yelling and screaming dissipated, Cleopatra went upstairs, picked up a suitcase she had packed earlier and left the house. She told Michael as she was leaving that she would seek a lawyer the first thing Monday morning and would have him physically removed from the house if necessary.

Pulling away from the house Cleo could see through the large picture window in the living room both sets of parents still arguing. Michael was sitting with his head bowed in both of his hands.

CHAPTER 20

"All Your Goodies Are Gone" . . . .

Attorney Marcie Fisher was one of the most sought after lawyers in her field. She specialized in divorce cases and represented only women. She was known as the "female ball crusher" and many a man was virtually brought to tears after she broke him down and emptied his wallet. Her colleagues referred to her as a man-hater and her female clients praised her as their Queen of the Amazons. According to her, the only thing a man was good for was donating his seed for babies and all men should be kept in a cage until needed for hard labor or sperm donation. Standing six feet two inches in her stocking feet, many a man feared the wrath of one Marcie Fisher.

Sitting in Ms. Fisher's office, Cleopatra looked around at the lavish furnishings and the expensive paintings on the walls. She was amazed at the color scheme of the room and wondered just who did such wonderful decorating. The cool colors gave a calming effect to the senses and the pictures on the walls were all of women in various roles of domination. As she looked at each picture, she realized they were all painted by the same woman—Marcie Fisher. Chuckling to herself, she immediately knew she

Mercedes M. Alexander

had come to the right place. This woman truly believed her calling was to annihilate the male species.

"Mrs. Beavers," the young receptionist was nodding her head toward Cleopatra, "Attorney Fisher will see you now. Please follow me."

Leaving the reception room and walking down the wide hallway towards Marcie Fisher's office, Cleopatra noticed only women working in the seven or eight impressive offices she passed. Each of the women wore dark business suits and appeared to be on top of her game. The offices looked and had the feel of success and Cleopatra was impressed by everything she saw, it gave her an instant feeling that this office would get down to taking care of business.

At the far end of the hallway was a wide set of double doors with elaborate engravings. The receptionist push the doors open and sitting behind a desk that had duplicate designs on the front as that of the double doors was Marcie Fisher. At first glance Cleopatra thought she was a woman who looked as if she could be anybody's sister or best friend but when she stood up to extend her hand, Cleopatra quickly changed her mind. The woman looked larger than life being as tall as she was and had hands the size of any pro basketball player. Her build was slim and she had her hair pulled back in a tight bun. Cleopatra's first impression was—transvestite.

The meeting with Marcie Fisher proved to be very productive. Cleopatra never knew how fed-up she was with Michael's bullshit until she began telling her lawyer the entire story from the beginning up to the day she finally left him. The entire time Cleo was talking Attorney Fisher was taking notes and nodding her head, not one time did she interfere with Cleo's story. Marcie let Cleo get everything off her chest and vent as much as she needed so that she would know that someone was listening and did care.

"Well, I think that sums up the whole sordid story Ms. Fisher."

Feeling a little uncomfortable about baring her soul to a stranger, Cleo had picked all the finger nail polish from the fingers on her left hand.

"I tried to be a good wife and did everything I could to help Michael when he had his heart attack, only to be paid back by finding out about his infidelities and a baby born to one of his mistresses."

The tears then started to fall and Cleo quickly fell apart in the attorney's office.

"Ms. Beavers, don't think you're the only woman to experience betrayal from your husband. I could tell you horror stories about the husbands of some of my clients. Your husband is still in pre-school, I know some bastards that have PhD's in screwing around. However, I will be more than happy to represent you and I promise you will come out on top of this. Most of the judges don't play around with men who sleep all over town and expect their wives to forgive them. You have a slam dunk case and have nothing to worry about. I need to ask you a few pointed questions and I need truthful answers from you. Do you feel like continuing this visit or do we need to do this another time?"

"I'm sorry about the display of emotions, this is the first time I've really sat down and had a good cry about my separation and the reason for it. Please, go ahead with your questions, I would like to end this marriage as soon as possible."

Ms. Fisher beckoned for her secretary and told her to get a tape recorder so that they would have a record of their conversation.

Mercedes M. Alexander

"Now Ms. Beavers, I want you to relax and I also want you to state verbally that you approve of the recording of this conversation."

"Yes, I approve of the recording of this conversation."

"Good, now let's began."

Marcie Fisher started the questioning by stating the date and the time the recording began. She gave the names of all the people in the office who were witness to the taping of the conversation and stated that the case was Cleopatra Handy Beavers vs. Michael Andrew Beavers, wherein Mrs. Beavers was petitioning the court for a divorce. The questioning went on for about an hour, Marcie Fisher was quite thorough with her little inquisition of Cleo. Cleopatra felt as if every aspect of her marriage had been questioned and discussed, there were no rocks left unturned.

"That's all I have to ask you for now Ms. Beavers. Please make an appointment with the receptionist to meet with me two weeks from today. I will do all the paperwork and have the divorce petition filed and Michael served by the end of this week. Let's see how fast we can push this through so you can get on with your life."

"Thank you Ms. Fisher, I do want this to end quickly," stated Cleopatra. "I need to move on and put all of this behind me."

The two women shook hands again and Cleo left the offices feeling as if a ton had been lifted off her shoulders. She did not want to see or talk with Michael anytime in the near future and would let her lawyer handle everything from this point. The very last thing Marcie Fisher said to Cleopatra was to advise her to visit her physician and get herself checked out. If Michael had impregnated one of the women, chances were he was lax in using condoms. She wanted Cleo to be sure that Michael had not passed any disease on to her while he was parking his little pecker in every vagina garage that had an automatic door opener.

*   *   *

Michael had moved out of the house three days after Cleo asked him to do so. At the insistence of Rev. Handy, he did not attempt to contact Cleo and took only his personal belongings from the house. He was now living in the garage apartment attached to his parent's home. Mrs. Beavers was constantly checking on him, she worried that he would have a setback because of the stress and strain from the break-up. Little did she know, Michael was already moving on with his life. The few times he told her he wanted to take a drive to clear his head, gave him the perfect opportunity to visit one of his lady friends. He had not changed his ways, he only became smarter about how he needed to play the game.

It could not be said that Michael did not love Cleopatra. He loved her in his own way and was happy and proud that she was his wife. However, he always felt that he could do as he pleased as long as he didn't get caught. Michael was addicted to sex, he liked it often and with as many different women as he could get it from. He told his close friends of his outside women and how he occasionally bought nice gifts to keep them on his leash. His prey was always a younger woman who looked up to him as a father figure and did exactly as he wanted them to do. All of them knew he was married and a few of them actually knew Cleopatra. Some of them opted to play his game because they were sure they could win him over and make him leave his wife. However, there were a handful of women who were downright bitches, they liked screwing married men because

Mercedes M. Alexander

there was no real attachment and they could do just as they pleased by having other boyfriends. Michael never knew he was playing with fire. Younger women usually only wanted an older man for what he could give them, when they wanted some real loving they made their way to a younger man. Such was the case with Michael and most of the women he thought he had control over. Michael was soon to learn how vicious a woman could be when she found out he had been cheating. The old saying "you can cheat on your wife but not on your woman" is a very true statement and Michael would eventually experience the wrath of one of the spurned women.

*   *   *

After leaving her attorney's office, Cleopatra decided to stop at one of the supermarkets on her way home. As she strolled through each aisle and slowly filled her basket she ran into Poopie. Happy to see her little friend, Cleo gave him a hug and told him how she missed being at work and would be returning soon. Poopie of course, gave her the lowdown on the office gossip and told her about the general manager being given the boot by the corporate office. He suggested that she return to work as soon as possible because everyone was flying by the seat of their pants and nobody knew who would be the new GM. He told her the corporate office wanted to replace the old GM with someone who was familiar with the city and the hotel and it was a possibility that someone within their office would be offered the job. Cleo was troubled about the news and decided she should return to work as soon as possible. The last thing she needed with a divorce in the making was to be left without a job. She would now have

Cleopatra's New Attitude

to support herself and be self-sufficient without a second income in her household. It would mean that money would be tight for a while, but she was determined to keep her house and try to keep her life as normal as possible.

Chapter 21

"Behind every dark cloud . . . ."

The divorce was not as easy as Cleopatra wanted it to be. Michael had hired a lawyer who was in constant battle with Marcie Fisher. Michael was asking for the house to be sold and that he be given half of everything. He even wanted half of the dishes, towels and furnishings in the house. It was his contention that he paid for half of everything and he wanted everything that was due him. Michael had turned out to be a perfect asshole and was making Cleopatra's life miserable. Cleo wanted to snatch his eyeballs out and stick them up his behind so that he could see how big of an asshole he really was.

Returning to work and trying to keep some type of structure to her life, Cleopatra went through each day working until she was exhausted and returned home late in the evening having a quick supper and going directly to bed. Over the last few weeks she had shut out her friends and family. She preferred to lick her wounds in private and had decided not to resurface to the family and friend scene until she felt comfortable about discussing the happenings in her life. Knowing her friends, she was sure they were laying in wait to do whatever harm they could to Michael. Her parents would call and leave messages on her phone telling her they just wanted to know she was all right and in return, Cleopatra would call them only when she knew they were not home and leave a message saying she was doing fine.

Everyone in the office at the Marriott knew about the upcoming divorce. Rumors about an outside child had spread like wildfire and some of the women went overboard to be kind to Cleo. Her biggest supporter during all of this was Poopie. Knowing his friend was hurting, he made sure she did not eat lunch alone and became her personal bodyguard during her working hours. Cleo was grateful to him because he never asked any questions, he was just always there to provide support.

Thinking she needed some time out of the office and feeling up to doing some socializing, Cleopatra decided to ask Poopie to accompany her to one of her favorite spots.

"Poopie, let's leave work at a normal time this evening and go out for drinks. I've decided to take my life off of hold and start living again. Do you think you can spare a few hours this evening and come with me?"

"Cleopatra, you must be reading my mind," was Poopie's exaggerated answer while waving his hands in the air and batting his eyes. "I know the perfect place for you to forget about everything and just have a good time. Now don't ask any questions, after work I'll follow you home so you can hop into my car and then I'll drive you to my favorite spot of heaven!"

Laughing at her friend and not wanting to squelch his bubbly spirit Cleo agreed to go with him.

*　　*　　*

Cleopatra's New Attitude

Poopie was driving like a bat out of hell. His little red 1974 Porsche made Cleopatra feel as if she were riding in a toy race car while sitting almost on the ground. All during his speedway driving, Poopie explained to Cleo that his car was the ultimate. He had had the car refurbished and the car sported antique license tags. She had to admit that it was a showpiece and very flashy.

They finally roared up to Poopie's surprise spot. The pink flashing sign outside of the club read "The Closet Club" and there were men and women standing in line wanting to get into the place.

"This seems to be a popular place Poopie, I don't think I've ever heard of it. Do you come here often?"

"My friend owns this club and I come here three or four times a week. Just wait until you see the dance floor and the furnishings. This place is going to blow your mind!"

Poopie did not lie, the place really did blow Cleopatra's mind, especially when she realized she was in a gay bar. There were men dancing with men and women dancing with women. Everyone in the place knew Poopie and a few of the men gave Cleopatra a disapproving eye.

"Come on Cleo, let's give it a whirl on the dance floor." Poopie extended his hand and practically drug Cleo to the middle of the dance floor.

Cleopatra had not danced in ages and was a little uncomfortable. Poopie on the other hand was a pro, his moves and gracefulness on the dance floor amazed her. Finally, she calmed down and started to feel the music and she danced with Poopie for the next thirty minutes.

"Oh Poopie, I'm having so much fun. Thank you for bringing me here, this place is on fire!"

Mercedes M. Alexander

"Well, if a woman wants to have a good time with no strings attached she should always hookup with a gay man. We can take you to the moon and back all in the name of having a good time and only want friendship. If you go out with a straight guy and he spends a little money on you he wants you to let him cash in his booty coupons. Gay men are not like that, when we're your friend we stick with you and will always have your back."

Laughing at Poopie, Cleo had to wipe tears from her eyes. "Poopie, only you would come up with the phrase "booty coupon" and at this point in my life I don't think any man would want to cash in any coupons I would be handing out even if I said it was double coupon week. I have such a sour taste in my mouth about romance right now and I would probably chop a man's head off if he even tried to approach me."

"Give yourself some time Cleo. Your pain is still fresh and you're right in the middle of a divorce. Let's sit back in the corner and talk, it might do you some good to let out some of your anger. I promise whatever you tell me will stay between the two of us—just use me as a sounding board. Once you let it out, I guarantee you will feel better."

Looking at her friend and feeling secure with him Cleo decided to take him up on his suggestion and bend his ear.

*   *   *

The next day at work members from the Marriott Corporate Office in Washington, D.C. were buzzing around the offices. The announcement that there was an opening for a new GM at the hotel had been posted for more than three weeks and qualifications needed to apply for the job were explicit. The corporate office personnel department made it quite clear if you did not meet the qualifications as posted there was no need of you applying for the job. When all was said and done, Cleopatra was the only person qualified to even apply for the position. All the other supervisors who had been there for years did not meet the educational requirements and none of them had bothered to take any of the training courses offered to them over the years. Cleo on the other hand had all of the educational qualifications and over the years had applied for and taken every course offered and had been certified in three areas of the hospitality industry.

Sitting at her desk working on contracts for an upcoming event, Cleopatra was approached by Jimmy Beaks the head of the personnel team from D.C. He stood over her with a smile on his face and carefully looked around her office at the plaques on her walls.

"It seems that you have been very busy over the years Ms. Beavers. From the looks of all the certificates and plaques on your walls, you qualify for working in our corporate offices. I know you did not apply for the GM job but we were given a high recommendation from one of your co-workers who wanted us to consider you for the position. According to him, you know the ins and outs of this business like the back of your hand. Would you please meet with me for lunch today? I would like to have a chance to talk with you and explain the dilemma we are facing while trying to keep this hotel viable in the market. It may prove beneficial to you and your co-workers if you just sit with me for a while and let me make my pitch. I assure you that my instructions to talk with you come from a high source in the company and I am following orders."

Stunned by the abrupt statement made by Jim Beaks, Cleopatra only nodded her head to give him the OK that she would join him for lunch.

Mercedes M. Alexander

"Good then, I'll meet you in the hotel restaurant at 12 noon. I've already had a table reserved in one of the private dining rooms, I think our conversation should be kept just between us for now."

As Jim walked away Cleo dropped her pen and stared in his direction. Did she hear him correctly? Did he just say to her that the hotel had a dilemma and she needed to talk to him not just for herself but for the benefit of her co-workers? Something strange was brewing and to find out what was happening she would have to talk with Jim Beaks.

"Hey, didn't I just see funny looking Beaks leave your office?"

Poopie was taking candy from Cleo's candy jar and making himself at home in the chair reserved for clients.

"You know that he's been sniffing around here for a few days and has not really spoken to any of us. He has had a look of disapproval on his face since he walked through the front doors and most of us think he disapproves of how we've been running things around here. The last person we need to piss off is chicken face Beaks, you know he cleaned house at one of the Marriott's in Texas and I wouldn't put it pass him to do it here."

"Oh stop your whining Poopie, from what I heard they needed to clean house. We're top notch here and have customer satisfaction ratings that are very high. I'm not really worried about them cleaning house. However, he did say something to me that has me a little disturbed. We're meeting for lunch in about forty minutes, so after work come by my house and I'll give you the 411 on our conversation."

Poopie's mouth dropped. "You mean he invited you to lunch. You know he's not married and he just might be looking for poontang on the side. Just make sure that your booty coupons come with a high price!

Cleopatra's New Attitude

Cleopatra could not help but laugh at her friend, she knew he was only joking and being his usual funny self.

"Alright, you've said enough. Now get out of my office and I'll see you this evening. In the meantime, keep this conversation to yourself."

Poopie left with Cleopatra still wondering just what her meeting would be about.

*   *   *

Sitting at lunch with Jim proved to be a very pleasant experience. He was quite charming and very witty. Cleopatra was quickly put at ease with him and enjoyed his company. It would be forty minutes into the lunch before Jim dropped his bomb and it was a very large bomb.

"Cleopatra, I have been authorized to offer you the GM job. I know you did not apply for it and I believe that the reason you didn't apply was because you thought you would be wasting your time. Believe me when I say you are more than qualified and you have come highly recommended by some prominent people in the community who have ties with the corporate office. I know this comes as a shocker, so I want you to take tomorrow off so you will have a three day weekend to think about this before you give me your answer. Please know that I will do everything in my power to help you be successful in this job and I really would like to see you accept this challenge."

Floored by the offer, Cleopatra almost choked on her lunch. She quietly put her fork down and stared into Jim's face.

"You're serious aren't you? In my wildest dreams I would never have believed that I would be offered a job as GM for a Marriott property. This is quite flattering Jim, please let me think about this over the weekend and I promise to get back to you Monday morning with an answer."

Jim stood and shook Cleo's hand and stated that he looked forward to her answer on Monday. Cleo then exited the restaurant walking on a cloud with a huge grin on her face.

I've been offered the GM job, oh my God.

Chapter 22

"Still waters run deep . . . ."

Leonard had kept himself busy over the last few months by volunteering at the church and spending as much time as he could with Matthew. He knew all about Cleo and her divorce proceedings because he had hired a private investigator to keep an eye on her and to report to him weekly. If he could not be near her, he would protect her from afar. He also hired two private bodyguards to watch Cleo's house from sundown to sun up just in case Michael decided to show his face. Leonard knew about all the women Michael had had in his life and he also knew about the three new ones. The last woman Michael hooked up with was aiming for a wedding ring and had made threats about just what she would do to him if she caught him screwing around. Of course, Michael took her warnings with a grain of salt but Leonard knew the history of the woman and also knew that Michael was flirting with danger.

Matthew had become a permanent fixture in Leonard's life. He was with him just about all the time and had started spending nights with him during the week. He now playfully called Matthew "son" and Matthew's new name for him was "pops". Spending week nights with Leonard meant

Mercedes M. Alexander

that Leonard had to get up early to get Matt ready for school and drive him there. Leonard loved every minute of being the "parent" and had made up his mind to talk with David and Esther Allen about adoption.

"Alright son, you need to go into the kitchen and park your behind in a chair at the table until you finish your homework. When you're done, bring it to me so I can check it. If you do well, we'll go over to the ice cream shop and buy that tutti-frutti stuff you like."

"Give me an hour Pops and I'll be ready to roll. I don't have a lot of homework tonight. We have a substitute teacher in that class until Mrs. Cook comes back from having her baby.

"Do a good job Matthew and take your time."

"Sure Pops—I'll be ready to go in an hour."

Leonard decided to go into his office and check his e-mail and maybe do a little work while Matt did his homework. His first e-mail was from Jim Beaks, it read:

> Offered the job to Cleopatra Beavers. You were right, Cleopatra is very qualified and is on top of her game. Since we have been needing to hire minority GM's, she would make the perfect choice. I have given her until Monday to give me her decision. I think she'll bite the worm, she seemed interested.
>
> Will keep in touch.
>
> Jim

Good job Jim, thought Leonard. *She is the best candidate for the job and we'll all make sure she's successful.*

Cleopatra's New Attitude

*   *   *

"Aw Pops, can't we get at least a gallon of the stuff. You claim you don't like it but the last time you ate your half and then started on my half."

Leonard chuckled and rubbed the small boy on the top of his head. "I guess I can eat as much as I want since I'm paying for it. But since you want to play the stingy game we'll go ahead and buy half a gallon of tutti-frutti."

While paying for the ice cream and keeping an eye on Matt, Leonard's attention was diverted to a scene being displayed very loudly in public. It was Michael Beavers standing in the doorway of the ice cream parlor with two very irate women belittling each other verbally. Michael seemed amused by the scene and had the audacity to make the statement that they need not fight over him because there was enough of him to go around. Instead of turning their anger toward Michael for making such a callous statement, the women continued to yell at each other about who Michael really wanted. Since there was only one door to come in and out of at the shop, Leonard ushered Matt to a corner and took a seat and watched the ongoing display of foolishness. After three or four minutes of bantering back and forth, one of the women took a swing at the other and the fight was on. The manager of the shop had already called 911 to report a problem and ask for police assistance and three minutes into the fight a squad car pull over to the curb. Both women were arrested while Michael just stood there and told the officers that he tried to stop the fight but could not handle the two women. Leonard shook his head knowing that Michael had told a bold face lie, Michael had never lifted his hands to stop anything.

Mercedes M. Alexander

Michael walked over to the counter of the ice cream shop and sat on a stool close to Leonard and Matthew. He knew they had witnessed the fight and had probably heard the entire conversation between the two women. He turned to Leonard and Matthew with a sly smile on his face.

"Man did you see that, women are crazy around here. I guess it's true that there are five women to every man in Memphis. I'm kinda of getting tired of running from them but what can I say, they all seem to be attracted to me."

Listening to Michael was making Leonard sick to his stomach. The conceited bastard was actually bragging about the women fighting over him.

"Come on son, we've seen enough foolishness for one night." Leonard quickly grabbed Matt's hand and led him past Michael out the door.

"Pops, that man was stupid. Granny always told me that a man should respect a woman and if you didn't then you weren't a man. Have you ever had women fighting over you?"

Leonard was a little shocked by the child's statement. "Not quite Matt, and your granny was right, if a man has women fighting over him that means he's less than a man. If he has his business straight there should only be one woman in his life and she should be cherished." Feeling a little ashamed of himself because of his philandering past, Leonard tried to change the subject but to no avail.

"Well Pops, why don't you have a lady in your life? We could be the perfect family, a daddy, a mother and a child. Wouldn't that be great?"

"Right now young man you're all I can handle in my life right now. If God wants me to have a lady in my life, I trust that he will place her

Cleopatra's New Attitude

there. Now let's please change the subject and get home before this ice cream melts."

Heading for the car, Leonard's heart was a little heavy. Cleopatra was the only woman he wanted and he was uncertain as to whether she would ever give him another chance. It's not that he did anything wrong, it was that stupid kiss. He wondered if she had heard anything more about his scarlet past. If the truth were to be known the story of his life should start with "Once upon a time" . . . .

CHAPTER 23

"Standing in the shadow of love . . . ."

Cleopatra did just as she promised. After work she sat with Poopie and told him every detail of her lunch with Jim Beaks. He was ecstatic with the news and encouraged her to take the job. She mentioned to him that Jim talked about a prominent person in the community with ties to the corporate office recommending her for the job. She had no idea who this person was, and felt grateful that anyone thought she was competent enough to be a GM for such a prestigious hotel. Talking until midnight, Poopie reminded Cleo that she had the next three days off to ponder her offer while he had to be at work bright and early the next morning. He said his goodbyes and headed for home a little after midnight.

Sitting alone in her kitchen, Cleo was starting to see a rainbow at the end of her tunnel. With the GM position, she would be making four times more than she now made and could afford to buy Michael out and give him every damn thing in the house if he wanted it. This was an opportunity for her to make a fresh start and she knew she would walk into the office on Monday with a "yes" plastered to her lips when she talked with Jim.

Mercedes M. Alexander

*   *   *

Early Saturday morning, Cleo made calls to her girlfriends asking them to join her for brunch at her house at 10:30 a.m. Since she had made herself scarce the last month, they were eager to see their friend and find out how she was handling the upcoming divorce. Cleo also made a call to her parents and apologized for missing in action. They understood and wanted her to know they were just worried about her and hearing her voice made them feel better. She then told them about her job offer and that she believed this was going to be a new beginning for her. Rev. Handy was so excited he almost hyperventilated and told her not to ever forget when God closes one door, He opens another. This little revelation only made Cleo smile, she knew it was true.

By 10:45 a.m. the kitchen of Cleopatra Beavers was rocking with laughter and jokes. She had missed her friends and now they were all trying to make up for lost time. They drank wine and had broccoli, ham and cheese quiche. The Saturday morning blues was blasting from the radio and the "Golden Girls" were in full swing.

"I can't tell you how much I missed you heifers, I didn't know how closely I was connected to you guys." Pat giggled but Cleo went on with her speech. "It's almost as if nobody cut our umbilical cords and we were all attached. Thanks for coming over today. This is going to be the start of a new life for me and I want you all to be the first to know."

Cleo told about her lawyer, Michael's demands and the new job offer. Her friends immediately gave her a high five about the new job and started talking about what should be done to make sure that Michael didn't get any more than he took with him. They all agreed when the judge was told

Cleopatra's New Attitude

of his womanizing and the baby, the ball would be in Cleo's court and she could then call the shots.

"Look ladies, I don't want to fight about stuff in this house. With the promotion, I will be able to hire a decorator and gut the entire house. When I finish, you won't know the place. It will be as if Michael never lived here or ever existed."

"That's the attitude to take," exclaimed Annette. "The old saying, "You don't miss your water until your well runs dry" will hit Michael right between the eyes. He'll be real disgusted with himself when he sees how you picked up the pieces and move on with your life."

The party lasted until 2 p.m. in the afternoon. The only reason they stopped was because choir rehearsal was scheduled for 6 p.m. and they needed to make sure they did not walk into the church with liquor on their breaths. Had it not been for that fact alone, they probably would have been partying until late that night.

* * *

Sitting in the choir stand on Sunday morning and saying amen to the Pastor's comments, Cleo noticed two police officers standing at the back doorway talking to Kathy.

Lord, I wonder who they're looking for this time. The last time they showed up, somebody had stolen a car from the church parking lot. Seeing them here could only mean trouble, thought Cleo.

Kathy stepped outside with the officers and Annette glanced at Pat and Cleo with raised eyebrows. Something was wrong, they could see Kathy put her hands to her head and stare up toward the choir stand.

Mercedes M. Alexander

Then one of the ushers came forward and summoned the Pastor to come outside during the offering.

Ten minutes later a note was passed for Annette, Pat and Cleo to step outside. The three of them were visibly nervous. What was happening and why did all three of them have to step outside. When they approached Kathy, she immediately ran to Cleo and put her arms around her. In her panic Cleo started yelling wanting to know if something had happened to one of her parents.

The stocky officer grabbed Cleo by the arm and led her to a chair. "Mrs. Beavers, as far as I know your parents are fine. Your husband, Michael Beavers, was found dead about an hour ago by a maid at a small motel on Elvis Presley Blvd. We need you to come with us to identify the body."

Cleo was numb, she couldn't cry, she couldn't ask questions, all she could do was stare and allow herself to be led outside the church by her girlfriends as they all headed for the city morgue.

*   *   *

Identifying Michael's body was not an easy task. Whoever decided to butcher him had also taken the knife to his face a number of times. The investigator from the scene of the crime said he had seen this many times and that this was a crime of passion. Somebody was angry enough with him to stab him over and over again. Pat was the one to identify the body and Kathy agreed. The watch that was found on the body had Michael's name engraved on it and had engraved on the back "From Your loving wife, Cleo."

Cleopatra's New Attitude

*   *   *

Monday morning was a nightmare. The Commercial Appeal had a headline that you would normally see in a rag paper. "Well Known High School Football Coach Found In Seedy Motel Stabbed To Death" was the headline with an article that made Cleo's stomach turn. Out of decency, she got dressed quickly that morning and headed for his parent's house. She still had not shed a tear. She was mad about the fact that Michael lost his life in a room at the local hoochie hotel and now everybody knew his business.

Mrs. Beavers met Cleo at the door and wailed for fifteen minutes. The woman was inconsolable and Mr. Beavers was walking around as if he were in a trance. Rev. and Mrs. Handy arrived five minutes after Cleo and quickly took over calling people and making arrangements for the funeral. They were told that Michael's body would not be released from the crime lab for four to five days so they made plans for a funeral on the following Saturday. It had not dawned on Cleo that she was now a widow.

*   *   *

Upon hearing about the tragedy, Jim Beak called Cleo on her cell to let her know he would wait on her answer and for her to take all the time she needed to work through her grief and get her business taken care of. In the meantime, Jim would remain in town and be acting GM for the hotel.

*   *   *

151

Mercedes M. Alexander

Leonard was beside himself wondering how Cleopatra was handling the situation. He could not imagine the stress she must have been experiencing and wanted to be there for her so she would have him to lean on and know how much he really cared. He sent flowers to Cleo's home from his office and sat by the phone hoping she would call him. By Wednesday of that week, he could no longer contain himself. He had to see her so he took the chance and showed up on her doorstep at 10 a.m. that morning.

When Cleo saw Leonard she rushed into his arms and clung to him. Just the sight of him made her want to hold on forever, it was then the tears started.

"I knew you would come, I can't explain it but I felt it in my spirit that you would be here for me. Thank you for coming and excuse my outburst of emotion. Just seeing you makes me feel as if everything is going to be all right."

Leonard led Cleopatra into the living room. He could feel her essence in the room, it was a room that only Cleopatra could create. Antique furniture mixed with modern, fresh flowers placed strategically around the room, abstract art and walls painted in two contrasting citrus colors gave the room a relaxing feeling that should come with every home. While he held her close and rocked her as they sat on the sofa, Cleopatra wept softly and keep repeating over and over, "I knew you would come".

Cleopatra soon gathered her composure and started talking non-stop about what really happened between her and Michael. Although Leonard already knew the sordid details, he sat patiently and let her get everything out in the open. His only thought during her entire conversation was that she only knew half of what Michael had been doing and as far as he was concerned, she did not need to know more than she already knew.

152

Cleopatra's New Attitude

"Cleopatra, I've been purposefully keeping my distance and respecting your request that I keep away. But after this tragedy, I had to let you know that I deeply care about you and will be at your beck and call. I know you'll need to do certain things necessary for planning a funeral and although he had parents, you were still his wife legally when he died. There are a lot of things you will have to do, please let me make my office staff available to you for whatever you need. I have two accountants, a secretary who is a notary and a lawyer on retainer to help with any legal problems. At this point I really feel helpless because I just don't know what to say or do, but I want you to take your time and think about whatever you need and just let me know."

"Thanks Leonard, I will hold you to that promise. Right now I'm at a loss as to what I need to do. I haven't called my divorce attorney yet but I know she has heard about Michael's death. The newspapers made sure everyone in town knew about his death and the circumstances surrounding it. I just need a friend, someone I can confide in and know it will not go any further than between the two of us. My girlfriends are the best friends you could have, but we all tend to try to interject our feelings into every situation and I don't need that right now. I just need a willing friend who will lend me his ear and not judge."

For the next two hours Leonard and Cleo talked quietly about what had happened and what should be done. Their past indiscretion, which only consisted of a stolen kiss, was never mentioned and the two of them tipped around the issue. However, the sparks that were flying in the room between them could not be dismissed. Leonard felt as if she was his to protect and every time he touched her there was a tingling from his hand all the way to his chest. Cleo was getting the same vibes and felt more relaxed with him than she had been in months.

Mercedes M. Alexander

"You know Leonard, I just realized that I don't have to fight with Michael anymore about a divorce nor do I have to worry about buying him out of the house or dividing assets. It's so funny how life works—one minute you're up to your eyeballs fighting over silly things and the next minute God waves his hand and there's suddenly nothing to fight about anymore. I didn't hate Michael, I just wanted to be free of him once I found out about the many women he had had in his life. If Michael had made one mistake he could have been forgiven because we're all entitled to one but to make that mistake over and over again was unforgivable. I could never trust him again, he used women and I felt as if he had used me."

At a few minutes past noon, the doorbell rang. Without bothering to wait for an answer, Rev. and Mrs. Handy bounced through the door. They were surprised to see Leonard sitting in their daughter's living room but happy to see him. According to Rev. Handy, Leonard was an outstanding citizen and fast becoming one of the most respected men in his church.

"Well, fancy seeing you here Brother Leonard. I didn't know you knew our daughter, but I guess you know a lot of people in and around Memphis. How have you been doing? I didn't see you last week in church and had intended to give you a call but when all this happened, I just simply forgot. Good to see you son."

"Thanks Reverend", was the only reply Leonard made. He suddenly felt as if he had been caught with his hand in the cookie jar even though he had done nothing wrong.

Sensing Leonard's uneasiness, Cleo quickly picked up the conversation.

"Leonard and I have known each other for sometime Daddy. However, I didn't know he belonged to your church. That's real interesting, I guess I need to visit more often so that I'll know what's going on over there."

"Child, I don't want to hear nothing about you "visiting more often", you were born and raised in that church and you just need to bring your little behind back home where you belong. Mega churches such as the one you belong to are too impersonal and the minister doesn't have enough personal contact with his membership. Because you sing in the choir and lead most of the songs is the only reason your pastor knows who you are. I think being a member of a church that large is nothing more than wanting to be in the mix of what's happening now."

Jumping from her seat and reaching over to place her hand over her husband's mouth, Della Handy scolded him for being so outspoken. "Now you hush up old man, nobody asked you to preach a sermon on mega churches and now is not the time for you to be interjecting your thoughts where they are not needed."

Leonard and Cleopatra both laughed at the scene being played out in front of them. Although Della Handy was scolding her husband, she did it in a loving way and the two senior citizens looked at each other and chuckled. It was good to see two people who had weathered the storms of life and come out of them unscathed. While observing them, Leonard silently prayed to God that one day he and Cleopatra could be a couple growing old together and still in love like her parents.

CHAPTER 24

"Soon and very soon . . . ."

The funeral was planned for Saturday morning at 11 o'clock a.m. Cleo and her friends sat down with Mr. and Mrs. Beavers and created a beautifully written obituary for the newspaper and for the funeral program. Although Michael was probably burning in hell, if the words written on paper about him had been true he would have been given the job of gate keeper in heaven. Cleo felt a little skeptical about helping to write such a glowing account of Michael's life, but for the sake of his parents, she went along with the game. She had a problem with them writing that he had left behind a loving wife so she made them change the entire writing to 'he leaves to mourn his passing a wife . . . .' Mrs. Beavers did not like the fact that Cleo wanted the changes but under the circumstances, she understood just where Cleo stood. There was no mention of a child in the obituary and instructions were given to the minister to make the sermon brief—no longer than ten minutes. Cleopatra wanted to get this over with as soon as possible and move on with her life. She felt as if she could not tolerate anyone standing before the church congregation and lying about what a

Mercedes M. Alexander

wonderful person Michael had been when most of them knew that he lived most of his life perpetrating a fraud.

At precisely 11 a.m. the funeral director was leading Cleo and other family members into the church. The sanctuary was packed with extended family members, Michael's co-workers, ex-students, church members and people wanting to be nosey. The many flowers covering the front of the church made the coffin look small in size. On the top of the casket Cleo had a family spray that was made of Black-Eyed Susans, the cheapest flower the florist could find! Instead of wearing the traditional black dress of a grieving widow, Cleopatra entered the church in a beautiful pink and gray silk suit. All of the music chosen was upbeat and nobody would be allowed to give any short extemporaneous speeches about their friendship with Michael. The entire funeral should not last longer than thirty minutes. The funeral would be conducted with the casket closed and all remaining flowers after the funeral were to be taken to a local nursing home to be distributed to the residents.

Fifteen minutes into the funeral while the choir was singing the popular song "Going Up Yonder" a loud wail came from the back of the church. Then there was another wail on the other side of the church. Like a chain reaction, wailing started in almost every corner of the church. Taking her time and looking behind her, Cleo noticed young women crying and snotting as if they had lost their mothers. It then struck her that these were some of the "other" women in Michael's life. The whole thing became a circus scene as people in the congregation began to whisper about the women. It was quite clear that everybody in the church knew exactly what was going on. Michael's women had come to grieve for him. It was

Cleopatra's New Attitude

apparent that the women did not know about their other competition because some of them started staring each other down.

Looking to her right she noticed Mrs. Williams sitting on the other side of the church with little Alexis sitting in her lap. She had dressed the child in a peach colored dress with a little bonnet to match. The child looked like an angel and was sitting very quietly on her grandmother's lap. Mrs. Williams noticed Cleopatra staring at her and politely nodded her head. Cleopatra could not help but smile at the old woman and looked intently at the child while wishing she could have been her mother. Michael may have passed away from this earth but he left a constant reminder of himself in the form of that little girl. She was the spitting image of her father.

All during the sermon loud crying interrupted the minister. Cleopatra sat silently with her head held high and hoping the entire ordeal would soon end. Finally the minister finished his nine minute eulogy and the undertakers were hauling Michael's body out of the church to take it to its final resting place while his soul was surely trying to stump out the fires in hell. It was precisely 11:30 a.m.

While sitting at the graveyard Cleo looked over to her mother-in-law and could see the grief on her face. This was the only time during the funeral Cleo shed a tear, her tears were for Mrs. Beavers because the woman had aged 10 years in the last week grieving for her child. Leaving the cemetery, Cleo made a special effort to stay close to Mrs. Beavers just to let her know that she was sorry for everything and would be there for her if necessary. However, unbeknown to anyone, Cleo's plans were to get on with her life as soon as possible and erase Michael's memory from her mind.

Mercedes M. Alexander

As soon as the family car arrived back at the church for the "Black folks Repass", the director of the funeral home handed Cleo all of the cards taken off the flowers at the church. As she casually glanced through them, she realized that seventy-five percent of the flowers had been sent by women whose names were unknown to her. Her only thought was to thank the Lord that her episodes in life with Michael were now over.

Chapter 25

"Ain't no mountain high enough . . . ."

Getting back into her normal routine felt good to Cleopatra. She went back to work a few weeks after Michael's funeral and accepted the job as GM for the hotel. Her first action in her new position was to make Poopie her assistant. After flinging his arms and crying for a good five minutes, Poopie hugged Cleo and promised she would not regret her decision.

Cleo already knew she would never regret promoting Poopie. She had known for a long time that he was up on everything and everybody at the hotel. He had worked in just about every position there was in the hotel industry and all of the clients knew him by name and loved him. He probably would have been promoted to other positions a long time ago had he not been a gay man. Most of the men in management from the head office were uncomfortable with Poopie or any gay man for that matter and never took the time to see what a wonderful employee he had been. This would give him the opportunity to shine and shine he would. Her first directive to him was for him to come up with a plan to redecorate the offices and give it a more open feeling in the administrative area. Cleopatra knew he had a gift when it came to decorating and had

Mercedes M. Alexander

no doubt when people from the corporate offices visited they would take notice and ask about the decorator.

Keeping herself busy at work and rekindling her friendship with Leonard made her happier than she had been in years. Although she had gone out to dinner with Leonard a few times and talked with him constantly on the phone, the relationship had been above board and no stolen moments of intimacy had occurred between the two. There were a few times when Cleo wanted to take the lead to reach over and kiss Leonard but she felt that as a woman it would appear unladylike if she did so.

*   *   *

Leonard was just where he wanted to be—a part of Cleopatra's life with the possibility of getting closer as the weeks went by. He made sure he kept his hands to himself and was the perfect gentleman every time he and Cleo went out on a date. He arrive at her house and waited just inside the front door until she was ready to leave and he always walked her to the door after the date, never entering the house. He was really surprised at himself, there was no pressure to try to take the relationship to the next level and he was content with that.

Today was Friday and this would be a long weekend because of Memorial Day. Leonard had access to a yacht in Gulfport, Mississippi that belonged to one of his associates. Although he knew nothing about sailing, his friend told him there was a full staff on the yacht and he would not be using it for the month of May. Leonard thought this might be the perfect opportunity to take Cleopatra away from the city and let her relax.

Cleopatra's New Attitude

According to his friend the boat had four separate sleeping quarters with private baths, a dining area, lounge area and a deck that was fabulous. It also came equipped with a captain, two assistants, a cook and a butler.

Leonard decided to try his luck and extend an invitation to Cleo.

"Hello Cleo, how has your day been thus far?

"You must have had a little "ESP" this morning. I have been up to my neck in contracts, phone calls and employee disputes since I walked in the door at 8 am. This is one day I wish I could take off and forget about work for a few hours. What have you been doing?

Blowing a little air between his teeth, Leonard decided to bite the bullet and tell her exactly why he called.

"My day has been fine and I'm calling to see if you have any plans for this holiday weekend."

"Well no, I hadn't thought about doing anything for this weekend. If you want, I could get food together and we can have a picnic on Monday."

"I'm thinking a little more in terms of you and I taking a trip to get out of the city. I have a friend with a yacht and he's made it available to me for the next few days. You could have your own private room and the yacht is staffed, all you have to do is relax and enjoy yourself."

Cleopatra was grinning from ear to ear, this was too good to be true.

"Oh my God, I would love to go. When do we leave and what do I need to pack, I can't wait to get away from this city!"

"We leave tonight on a private plane so only pack fun clothes and maybe something to go out to dinner in while we're in Gulfport."

Mercedes M. Alexander

Leonard was ecstatic, this was going to be great. He would have Cleopatra all to himself for three whole days, his dreams were finally coming true.

"I'll pick you up at your house around seven, be ready!"

Oh, don't worry, I'll be ready. Just make sure that you're not late."

"Baby, this is one time I will be standing on your doorstep a few minutes before seven. I'll see you then, bye."

"Bye Leonard."

Hanging up the phone Cleo was beside herself wanting the day to quickly end. She thought of how much fun it would be to get away on a yacht and be alone with Leonard. It then dawned on her that he had referred to her as "baby". Normally she would have been indignant about him calling her such a name, but today she melted when his deep baritone voice referred to her as "baby".

*   *   *

Cleo raced home after work and packed as quickly as she could. She then took a quick shower and was dressed and ready to go at 6:45, the doorbell rang at 6:50.

Standing at the door with one yellow rose in his hand was Leonard dressed in khaki pants and a blue and yellow stripped Polo shirt. He immediately reached out his hand for Cleo as she opened the door and before he knew it she had thrown her arms around his neck thanking him for coming to her rescue and taking her away when she needed it most. Her face was so close to his that he could feel her warm mint smelling breath making its way up his nostrils. Without thinking, he wrapped his

Cleopatra's New Attitude

arms around her and began very slowly planting the most sensuous kiss on her lips. Instead of Cleo pulling back, she was holding on for dear life. Leonard's body was about to betray him and he tried to pull back but Cleo was not letting go and pressing herself closer and closer. Now he could no longer contain himself as he held her and explored her mouth with his tongue.

Cleopatra surprised herself at her response to him. Her body was fast becoming putty in his hands and her insides felt like jelly. There was something going on here that she had never felt, her body was betraying her and she wanted him as she had never wanted any man.

Leonard was the first to gain his senses and gently pushed Cleopatra away.

"Cleo, I think we need to cool this for now. I'm sorry if I held you too close or took advantage of the situation."

"Oh hush Leonard, you didn't take advantage of me. There's something here I need to explore and I can't wait to have you to myself. Don't think about putting me in a room alone on this trip. I think I want to stay as close to you as possible and let the chips fall wherever they may."

Cleo then gave him a seductive look and another kiss, but this time she let her tongue do the exploring.

Leonard had been caught off guard. After the extra kiss from Cleo he didn't know what to say or do so he just picked up her suitcase and motioned for her to follow him to the car. Once they were buckled up and backing out of the driveway Leonard looked over at Cleo and smiled.

Cleo smiled back at him and teasingly said, "What's the matter Leonard, Cat got your tongue?"

CHAPTER 26

"Tonight is the night . . . ."

At precisely 7:15 pm. Pat was calling Cleo to see if she wanted to run around and do a little shopping over the weekend. When Cleo's answering machine picked up, the message was, "Sorry I missed you. I'll be out of town for the weekend so try me again on Tuesday of next week. Ciao, Cleo."

Why that little heifer, I wonder just what she's up to. I don't remember her telling me she would be out of town this weekend, thought Pat. Feeling a little uneasy about the message, Pat immediately called Annette to see if she knew about Cleo leaving town.

"Annette, I just called Cleo's house and got this strange message about her being out of town, do you know anything about this?

Rising to turn the TV down so she could hear Pat, Annette thought she heard her say that Cleopatra had left town.

"Can you repeat that Pat, I thought I heard you say she had gone out of town. I just talked to her this morning and she said nothing about taking a trip. You must be mistaken because she would have let one of us know if she was going to be out of pocket for the weekend."

Mercedes M. Alexander

"You heard me right, she's out of town for the weekend according to her answering machine. Now I know she didn't just jump up and leave town without telling one of us and if you talked with her this morning and she didn't mention it, something must be wrong. I've never known her to leave town by herself all the years we've been friends."

Annette smiled into the phone, "Who said she left town alone? She could have a man friend we don't know about. Lord knows she deserves some happiness after having to put up with that asshole of a husband."

"Girl, she doesn't have a man friend and the only somebody that's been calling her and sniffing around lately is that no good son-of-a-bitch Leonard Wilkins. Aw, hell no, she wouldn't have gone on a trip with him, would she?"

"Well, from what I hear he knows his way around a woman's body and Cleopatra hasn't had any for almost a year. She knows he's a dog and if she is with him, more power to her. I could use a man to rock my world, especially one with money!

"You hussy," exclaimed Pat, "Don't you know that man could only mean trouble. What about all the other women he's been fooling around with? Do you think that dog would drop them so quickly and make himself a one-woman man? I swear I'll have him killed if he hurts her."

"Hold on Pat, Cleopatra knows exactly what kind of man he is. Maybe she just wants to have a little fun without strings attached. I feel sorry for Leonard Wilkins because if he is with Cleo, something tells me he's in for the ride of his life and Cleopatra is driving the vehicle."

"Think what you want, I'm still concern. I think I'll check with her parents to see if they know anything about her missing in action this weekend. If they could shed a little light on this mystery I would feel a lot better and not worry myself for the next three days."

"Do what you gotta do, call me back and let me know what you find and make sure you don't say too much and alarm her parents."

Annette then hung up the phone with a wicked smile on her face. *You go girl, get yours and have enough fun for me*, she thought.

Of course, Rev. and Mrs. Handy could not shed any additional light on the situation. They only told Pat that Cleo had called and said she was going out of town with a friend to get out of the city for the weekend. She had also told them that if they needed to reach her they could call her on her cell.

Call her on her cell huh, I guess that means she's not in trouble. Pat put the phone back into its cradle and said a silent prayer, *Lord, please let that girl keep her dress down, her legs closed and her panties up this weekend!*

* * *

Arriving in Gulfport at 8:15 p.m. gave Cleo and Leonard almost thirty minutes of daylight before darkness over took them. Leonard suggested they have the limo driver take them to have dinner at one of the casinos where they could sit and watch the sun go down. After dinner, they would then board the yacht and start their weekend adventure. The two of them had a wonderful candlelight dinner on a small private deck overlooking the ocean and Cleopatra was wishing this time would never end. Leonard was so handsome and attentive and made her feel as if she was the only woman in the world.

Mercedes M. Alexander

As dinner was cleared from their table, the music coming from the restaurant was a melody of favorite oldies but goldies. When the song "If This World Were Mine" began, Leonard stood up and extended his hand to Cleopatra. She immediately stepped into his arms and let him lead her in a slow love dance. When the music finished, Leonard whispered in her ear, "Let me make you happy Cleopatra, I promise that I will do everything in my power to never fail you. Let me love you, hold you, kiss you and always be by your side."

Looking into Leonard's eyes, Cleopatra could see a sincerity in the man that touched her heart. Without saying anything, she pressed her lips against his and clung to him while tears rolled down her cheeks. She had never been so happy.

"Hurry and get me to the yacht Leonard, I want you to hold me, kiss me and love me as I've never been held, kissed or loved before."

Leonard left a $100 dollar bill on the table and ushered Cleo from the restaurant. He could not get to the yacht fast enough.

*   *   *

The yacht was spectacular, never in Cleo's wildest dreams had she imagined being on such a boat with so much luxury. The Captain greeted them and introduced his assistants, the butler and the cook while they all stood at attention. The butler immediately grabbed their luggage and headed down the stairs to the sleeping quarters while the Captain gave them a tour of the yacht. It was larger than Cleo's house and very elegantly appointed. This was a yacht you could live on and never plant foot on dry land again, it was simply beautiful. After the tour, Leonard explained

Cleopatra's New Attitude

to the cook and the Captain that he and Cleo had just had dinner and both of them had had long days and would like to retire for the night. The Captain gave a nod and immediately one of his assistants appeared to escort them to their sleeping quarters.

The cabin door opened up to a sitting room decorated in animal prints and red leather. Upon entering the master bedroom, Cleopatra noticed the butler had placed all of their luggage in the one room. The room was huge with a round bed, a large picture window that gave them a private view of the ocean, an entertainment center with a huge TV and stereo system and an abundance of CDs with all types of music. The master bath was all marble with a round bathtub big enough for four people, a separate standing shower, his and her vanities and a bidet. There were vases of red roses placed in several areas of the bedroom which gave it a smell of romance.

"Oh Leonard, this is magnificent! I want to pinch myself to make sure I'm not dreaming."

"No baby, you're not dreaming, this is all very real and so am I. Why don't you make yourself comfortable and take a hot bath to relax. I'm going to talk with the Captain to find out exactly what our travel route is and I'll return in about thirty minutes if that's alright with you."

Cleopatra gave Leonard a peck on the cheek. "Don't stay any longer than thirty minutes—I'll be waiting for you."

Winking his eye, Leonard exited the room and whistled all the way up the stairs. All his wishes and wants were at hand and he would make sure that he did nothing to screw-up this relationship. He loved Cleopatra and tonight he would show her just how much.

CHAPTER 27

"She was a gypsy woman . . . ."

Thirty minutes later Leonard was knocking on the cabin door. He could hear music coming from the room but Cleo did not answer his knock. He decided to slowly open the door and ease into the room. When Leonard opened the door, he was surprised to see that the lights had been dimmed and candles lit different corners of the room. There were red rose petals making a trail from the door through the private sitting room to the door leading to the bedroom. When he entered the bedroom there was Cleopatra standing by the large window with two glasses of champagne in her hand. She was wearing a peach colored negligee that was made of layers and layers of incredibly sheer material. Her skin was shimmering with something unfamiliar to him and the perfume she was wearing had enveloped the room and was as enticing as hell. She smiled at him and beckoned for him to come closer.

"Cleopatra, do you know what you're doing?" exclaimed Leonard, as a low moan started coming from him.

"Of course I do Honey, this is our night to explore each other. We're both adults and I know exactly what I want you to do. Come here and stop talking."

Mercedes M. Alexander

Leonard slowly walked toward Cleo and took the champagne glasses from her hand. He took his hands and moved them very slowly caressing her face, took his finger and traced her lips, her nose, each ear and both eyes. Without ever taking his eyes from hers, he then began to let his hands travel over the womanly parts of her body. Her nipples stood erect as he played with them with his thumbs and as he ran his hands farther to her waist then her hips. Cleopatra closed her eyes and prayed that he would never stop.

"Baby are you sure you want to do this? I want nothing more than to make love to you until the sun rises, but you need to be sure this is what you really want."

Cleo opened her eyes and was touched that even in the heat of passion, Leonard was still more concerned about her feelings and not trying to force anything on her.

"I know what I want Leonard. I have never wanted a man before, not like the way I want you now." She then took his hand and led him to the bed.

Kissing Cleopatra passionately and exploring every inch of her mouth made Leonard tremble. He then kissed her neck and shoulders and felt her shudder under him. Standing to take his clothes off, he looked at her lying on the bed and prayed that this would be something wonderful for her. As he dropped his pants and climbed into bed, he slowly took the negligee from her body and marveled at how beautiful she was.

"I love you Cleopatra, I think I've loved you from the first night I saw you in that wonderful slinky silver dress. When I make love to you tonight, for me it will be a commitment, a commitment to love, honor and cherish you." Leonard then began his love journey, one that he had wanted for a long time.

Cleopatra's New Attitude

Cleopatra thought she felt the earth move as he made love to her. He had taken his tongue, worked his way around her entire body and showed her exactly what a man does when he loves a woman and wants her to experience nothing but pleasure. Never in her life had her body come so alive and experienced such a wanting. All she could do as he brought her from one height to another was coo and call his name ever so softly. His lovemaking was magical. Looking up at the ceiling above the bed, Cleopatra noticed for the first time a large mirror. She saw Leonard moving seductively while holding and making love to a woman, a woman she did not recognize, a woman who had the look of complete satisfaction on her face.

*   *   *

Opening her eyes from a deep sleep, Cleopatra began to remember what had taken place during the night in this wonderful soft round bed. She looked over at Leonard and noticed how young and peaceful he looked as he slept. As the sun put a soft shimmer of light in the cabin, Cleo took her hand and ran it along the perfect six pack of Leonard's chest.

My goodness, she thought, *I never believed I could feel such passion for a man and enjoy lovemaking as much as I did last night. I've lost a lot of time wondering just what I should feel during sex. Now that I know, I intend to experience it again and again and again with Leonard. Last night was absolutely beautiful!*

Leonard stirred in his sleep and Cleo watched him intently. She was so happy and content. Sliding closer to him, she put her head on his chest and her arm around him. Leonard was awaken by the movement in the

Mercedes M. Alexander

bed, he immediately reached for her and the lovemaking started again. This time Cleo played an active part by giving her all and making Leonard wish it would never stop. Leonard knew that he would one day give up everything to ask this woman to be his wife and hopefully, when the time came she would say "yes."

*   *   *

The next two days were filled with fun, laughter, relaxation and long nights of lovemaking. The two lovebirds were acting like newlyweds and could not keep their hands off each other. The crew members were very discrete and seemed to appear only when needed which gave them plenty of time alone to talk and discuss their intentions.

"You know Leonard, I feel silly saying this to you but I had never slept with any man other than Robert. I gave my virginity to him while in my senior year of college, got pregnant, lost a child and existed in a mediocre marriage for more than twenty years. I never had an orgasm or shuddered at a man's touch until the other night. It was amazing the way you made me feel."

Leonard had been listening intently and thought, *She's always been a good girl, not someone sleeping from man to man but a woman who is devoted to only one man. I cannot believe my blessing, God—please don't let me mess this up. I'm begging for your blessing that I can have a life with Cleopatra.* "Listen Cleo, you don't have to tell me anything that makes you feel uncomfortable. We can just start from this point and not look back. I'm perfectly happy with the way we are now and I want us to be committed to each other."

Cleopatra's New Attitude

Shaking her head and reaching for Leonard's hand, Cleo was determined to tell him everything. She got up, sat in his lap and began telling him her story from the time she met Robert until his death. She left no stones unturned and then confessed about the "Golden Girls" and their plot with Kathy at the restaurant.

Leonard roared with laughter when she finished. He could not believe that Cleo and her girlfriends had gotten the best of him. "So you're a mischievous little devil, I must confess I deserved every drop of that ice cream on both sides of my head!"

They both had a good laugh about the ice cream incident and discussed other things they though each should know. However, Leonard never told her about the hired bodyguards or the private detective.

"Since we're clearing the air to start our relationship on a clean page, I think I need to tell you something. I haven't always been an outstanding, upright man. I have gone through a lot of women in my life and I must confess that after I met you and joined church, I was ashamed of how I had lived. For the last six months, I've been on the straight and narrow with only one indiscretion. It was a mistake I could have avoided but was weak at the time and I've regretted it ever since."

"I don't want to hear about your indiscretions Leonard, I want to start fresh and leave the past behind us. You promised to be honest and faithful to me, that's all I need to hear. You told me you loved me and I believe you, please let the past and the women you were involved with be forgotten and let us move forward with our lives."

Sealing her statement with a kiss, Leonard could only smile with a sigh of contentment.

CHAPTER 28

"Yakety-Yak, Yakety-Yak . . . ."

The long weekend with Leonard ended much too quickly for Cleopatra. On Monday evening, she slowly packed her bags while looking around the cabin. This was where all her dreams had come true and she finally felt like a complete woman. Leonard had opened a door for her and once she had crossed the threshold into total fulfillment, she knew that she would never be satisfied with a mediocre love life again. This felt like the real thing and she kept pinching herself to make sure it was not all a dream.

"Baby, what's taking you so long to pack that one bag?" yelled Leonard from the front of the cabin. "You've been in there more than thirty minutes and I swear I haven't heard you move around in the room. Are you sure you're packing?

Sticking her head out of the door of the bedroom, Cleopatra threw a pillow at Leonard.

"Of course I'm packing, I'm just taking my time doing it. I don't want to leave this cabin but I know I have no choice. Promise me you'll bring me back to this same boat in the near future and work your magic again."

Mercedes M. Alexander

"Cleopatra, I'll bring you back to this exact spot as many times as you will let me. But now we have to leave, our plane leaves in less than an hour and it will take us thirty minutes to get to the airfield."

While leaving the yacht, Cleopatra took one last look at her floating miracle and thought, '*I now christen you "Cleo's Private Love Nest".*

* * *

Arriving back at Cleopatra's front door, Leonard timidly put her bag down and reached for her key. Cleo handed him the key and as soon as he had opened the door and placed her bag down she pounced on him. Taking her arms and locking his head close to hers, she slid her tongue in his mouth and slowly wiggled as close to him as she could.

The passion was building right there in the foyer of her home when the doorbell rang. Startled that anyone was even at her front door made Cleo swear under her breath. This was the most inopportune time for anyone to visit. She pulled herself from Leonard and slowly answered the door. Standing at the door was her neighbor's ten year old little girl, Sabrina.

"Good evening Mrs. Beavers, I saw you drive up and wanted to come over and give this to you. A lady came by yesterday and asked me to deliver this note to you. She said the front screen was locked and she couldn't slide it under the door. She even gave me five dollars to make sure I gave this to you as soon as you got home."

The child was beaming at what she thought to be her good deed. If she only knew what she had interrupted!

"Thank you Sabrina, now you run back home because it's getting dark and you don't need to be outside once the street lights come on."

180

Cleopatra's New Attitude

The little girl smiled and ran toward her home leaving Leonard and Cleopatra standing in the doorway watching.

"OK baby, I think that was an omen that I need to leave."

"Oh, do you really need to go? I could make us some coffee and we could find a movie to watch."

"Now Cleopatra, we both know if I stay five minutes longer, we'll be up the stairs in your bed. I think I need to leave, but I promise to call you as soon as I get home. OK?"

Not wanting to agree with him, Cleo knew he was right and reluctantly agreed. Giving him a quick peck on the check, she watched him as he walked to his car and stood in the doorway waving until he was out of sight.

Heading up the stairs, Cleo remembered the envelope delivered by her little neighbor and opened it. It was a note from Pat saying she needed to talk with her as soon as she got home and the word urgent was highlighted.

*   *   *

"Hello girlfriend," was the cheery greeting Cleo gave Pat as she answered the phone. "I got your message when I arrived back home this evening. What's so urgent?"

Sitting in her kitchen sipping tea, Pat noticed the unusually happy tune in Cleo's voice. "I just wanted to know when you got back to town and to make it a point to chump on your behind for not letting me know that you were going away for a long weekend. Don't you know I worry about you when I don't hear from you? Cleo you just jumped up and left town, and leaving the way you did sent alarms off. Annette didn't know where you were and your parents were vague about your whereabouts. I distinctly got the impression while I was talking with them that they had no idea where you were."

"Hold up Pat, I'm sorry I didn't call to let you know that I was going out of town, but it all happened so fast I barely had time to pack and give my parents a call. Let's just cut the chase and I'll tell your nosey behind exactly where I was and who I was with," chuckled Cleopatra.

"Cleopatra Beavers, this is not funny. If you think that disappearing for a weekend without letting someone know exactly where you're going and who you're going with is something to laugh about, we need to have a serious talk."

Twirling the telephone cord through her fingers, Cleo still had that blissful look on her face. "Alright, I'll tell you exactly where I've been, I went on a mini-vacation with Leonard."

"Good Lord, you'd better not mean Leonard as in Leonard Wilkins. We both know what kind of man he is and you don't need to go there. You need to have your head examined if you spent a weekend with him and please tell me you didn't sleep with him."

"As a matter of fact, I did go with the notorious Leonard Wilkins. He turned out to be a very sensitive man and whether or not I slept with him is my personal business."

The phone went dead. Cleopatra did not know if Pat had hung up in her face or if they had just been disconnected. *Whatever,* she thought, *I didn't really feel like explaining myself to Pat. She would never understand and never let up on me if she knew what really happened.*

Cleopatra's New Attitude

Walking into her closet to look for her robe, Cleopatra was reminiscing the last few days of her life. They had been quite glorious if she had to say so herself. The phone interrupted her thoughts. *Damn, will that girl ever give up,* she thought.

"Hello, Cleopatra, I promised to call as soon as I arrived home."

It was Leonard and the just the sound of his voice made Cleopatra's heart flutter. It was funny how quickly he had turned her life around.

"Well, I'm happy to know that you're a man of your word. Would you call me in the morning and meet me for breakfast. I want to inform you of my conversation with Pat a few minutes ago. The note that was delivered by my neighbor's child was from her and she has a few issues about my whereabouts over the weekend."

"Ok sweetie, I'll give you a call early and meet you. In the meantime, get a good night's sleep and dream only of me."

"I will Leonard, good night."

*   *   *

While preparing for bed, Cleopatra's doorbell rang at exactly 11p.m. *I wonder who could be at my door at this hour.*

Looking through the peephole in her front door, Cleo saw who the mysterious night visitors were. Standing in the middle of the night on her doorstep while apparently in a heated argument were Pat and Annette.

Well, well, I wonder just what they're disagreeing about. Not being able to control herself, Cleopatra opened the door laughing.

"Good evening ladies, what brings you to my front door at such a late hour?"

Mercedes M. Alexander

Pushing the door open and letting themselves in, Pat walked straight into the kitchen and started making coffee.

"Cut the bullshit Cleopatra, we're here to talk some sense into your ass. You seem to have lost your mind and before you cut off your own head, we're going to try to save you from yourself."

"Save me from myself! Who died and left the two of you in charge of my life? I believe I have been a grown woman for quite some time and I can take care of myself. Just because the two of you are my lifetime buddies does not give you the right to start dictating to me what I should and should not be doing!"

Sitting at the kitchen table with her legs crossed and looking up at the wall, Annette seemed not to be interested in any of the conversation. Instead she was smiling to herself and seemed to be consumed in her own thoughts. She finally rose from her chair and walked over and gave Cleo a hug.

"Cleo, I'm so happy to see that you're getting on with your life. Little Miss Busy Body here, woke me up and insisted that I come with her to your house at this ungodly hour of the night. She seems to think you are cutting your own throat because you gave Leonard a little of your time and maybe a few of your cookies."

Cleopatra and Annette had a good laugh about Pat's inability to let Cleo live her own life, but they also understood that she was concerned about her friend.

"Look Pat, I appreciate you being concerned and always having my back. But, to tell the truth, I don't need your help in this situation. Since the two of you are here, I'll just sit down and tell you where I went, who I went with, and exactly what happened."

Cleopatra's New Attitude

After talking non-stop for twenty minutes giving them every detail of her trip, descriptions of the yacht and how attentive Leonard had been, Cleopatra finished her story and sat with a coffee mug in her hand and a huge smile on her face.

Pat sat with a look of astonishment on her face. Annette was grinning from ear to ear and nodding her head in approval of what Cleopatra had told them.

"You mean to tell me that you opened your legs and let that man have his way with you," yelled Pat when she finally came out of her trance.

"Pat, calm down! He didn't have his way with me, if the truth were to be told, I had my way with him and I enjoyed every minute of it," Cleo exclaimed as she gave Annette a high five.

"Cleopatra, you're turning out to be just like Kathy, just plain whorish." was the only comeback Pat could think of.

Annette could not take it any longer, she stood over Pat and pointed a finger at her. "Listen up little woman, this is a new day. Women don't have to sit around waiting for the right man to come along, we now have the option to go for what we want. Just because Cleopatra decided to go away for the weekend with any man and have a good time is a testimony to her being able to move on with her life. You on the other hand have decided to make yourself judge and jury and sentence her to being a whore. That's not right and now I see why you didn't invite Kathy to this meeting. You knew that she would side with Cleopatra and you thought I would side with you to keep the playing field uneven in your favor. Well girlfriend, I think Cleo has the right to do as she pleases and if Leonard Wilkins can rock her world in the way she wants, then she should go for it."

185

Mercedes M. Alexander

"For your information Annette, I didn't invite Kathy because she is in the same boat as Cleopatra. Unknown to you and Cleo, Kathy has been having casual sex with strangers and I think the girl is a nymphomaniac. As women we don't have to have sex just to make a man happy and we don't need it as much as people say we do."

Not to be thrown off course Annette stood up and put her hands on her hips.

"Girl, Cleo and I both know that you haven't had sex for more than a year. Now you know that's not good. I hope you're still open for business because you know what happens when you don't wear earrings for a year!"

Annette and Cleo roared with laughter.

Cleopatra exclaimed she didn't know that Kathy was so liberal with her love life. "I guess we need to salute her in the words of the seven dwarfs the next time we meet her and just say, Hi Ho—Hi Ho."

Laughing until tears ran from their eyes, Cleo and Annette agreed that Kathy's business was her business and unless she brought up the subject, they should all act as if they never heard a word.

However, Pat was still a little down on Kathy and started talking about all the diseases she could get from so much sex. The only thought that ran through Cleopatra and Annette's minds was that they needed to get Pat out more and find a man so she could get her groove on and leave everybody else's sex life alone. They both sat and let Pat go on and on until they could take no more. Annette finally pushed Pat toward the door and wished Cleopatra a good night while Pat continue her tirade of who was a whore and who needed saving.

CHAPTER 29

"What a man, what a man . . ."

Dressing for work on Tuesday morning, Cleopatra kept staring at her phone. *'Leonard promised he would call me early this morning. If he doesn't call me soon I won't be able to meet him and get to work on time,'* she thought. Just then the front doorbell rang. *Gosh, my house is like Grand Central Station. I wonder who could be at my door this early.*

Rushing down the stairs, Cleopatra did not bother to look out of the peephole before throwing open the door. To her surprise Leonard was standing posed with two large bags in his hands.

"My lady, your knight in shining armor is here with your breakfast," were the words spilling from Leonard's mouth as he stepped in to the house and headed for the kitchen.

Cleopatra was speechless and actually looked out the door to see if he really left his white horse outside on her driveway. She shook her head as she thought, *"what a man, what a man"*, and followed him into her kitchen.

Leonard was already busy in the kitchen setting up his breakfast surprise. He had stopped at one of the fancy deli shops near his home and picked up a breakfast fit for a queen. When Cleopatra sat at the table he presented her with a breakfast that consisted of bagels with cream cheese and smoked salmon, fresh fruit, imported coffee and freshly squeezed orange juice.

"Alright baby, dig in and when we're finished we can talk about whatever it was that had you peeved last night."

"Oh Leonard, I wasn't exactly peeved, I just felt as if I'm being placed under a magnifying glass by one of my friends and she thinks it's her business to scrutinize every move I make and try to tell me what I should and shouldn't do. I know she's just concerned and loves me, but I'm a grown woman and I know exactly what I'm doing. I just need her to be my friend and not my mother. To be honest with you, Pat comes down on me harder than my mother about my personal life."

Leonard was listening intently to Cleopatra and thought it was funny that she needed to discuss a problem she was having with one of her girlfriends with him. He decided to let her talk and get it out of her system, thinking once she had vented she would drop the subject and talk about something else. He was surprised that she kept going on and on and even more surprised when she told him that he was the root of the problem.

"Wait a minute Cleopatra, are you telling me that Pat is chewing on your ass because of me? What's up with her? Does she think I'm not good enough for you or that I will do something to hurt you?"

"She cannot forget all the gossip she's heard about your past history or the incident at the bar with Sasha. I believe she thinks I'm on the rebound after finding out my late husband was such a bastard."

Cleopatra's New Attitude

Standing to face Cleopatra and pulling her to her feet, Leonard wrapped his arms around her and held her close.

"Cleo, I don't think you're on the rebound. I truly believe that what we felt during our little trip and what we feel right now is real. Every time I'm near you I get a warm feeling all over and want to hold you and never let go. I love you baby and I'm never going to let go."

"I believe you Leonard and I don't want you to let me go. Now that you know my friend is on the warpath and you are the target for her anger do you think you can handle it. There's going to come a time when the two of you will come face to face and I don't want either of you to be uncomfortable."

"For you honey, I would put up with the devil himself. Now we both need to head off for work. Call me as soon as you get home this evening and I'm going to come and pick you up for dinner. Don't ask questions, this will be another surprise."

Cleo planted a long and sensuous kiss on Leonard's lips. "I can't wait, I promise to give you a call as soon as I get home."

On the way to work Cleopatra hummed every tune on her radio. They were all love songs played on WDIA Radio Station and were slow jams. Leonard, on his way to work had put a Johnny Guitar Washington recording in the CD player of his car and listened to the artist as he sang 'I got a girl and she so fine, Make me wanna swing from a grapevine, She don't know what a thing she's causen, Got me running around wanna holler like Tarzan!"

* * *

Mercedes M. Alexander

The work day was a breeze for Cleopatra. Poopie had proven to be one of the best assistant's anyone could want. He not only kept Cleopatra abreast of everything going on at the hotel, he made it a habit of whipping the other employees in line whenever they seemed to be slacking off. Although Poopie was the ultimate watchdog, he did not make any enemies while doing so. Being a gay man, he had been ostracized most of his life because of his lifestyle. Poopie had come to realize in his early adult life that people needed to be handle with care and tact. He knew how to always prove his point without offending people and had developed this skill into an art.

"Boss lady, I have your complete agenda for tomorrow here. You have a meeting in the morning with the Physician's Association at 9 a.m. and a luncheon meeting with one of the vendors wanting our restaurant to use his services for cleaning supplies. These are the two most important items, everything else can be done whenever you decide to get to them."

"Thanks Poopie, I appreciate you keeping me on task and how many times do I have to tell you not to call me "Boss lady? You know I don't like it and I believe you keep on calling me that to rub it in."

Snapping his fingers and scurrying out the door, Poopie laughed at Cleo.

"Girlfriend, you know you got it going on and I'm just acknowledging it. Besides, it pisses two of your male employees off when they hear me say it. You know they both thought they would be in line for this job just because they were male and White. I think it completely floored them when they were told they did not even qualify to apply for the position and they're still in shock. Anyway, I need to keep saying it so they will remember who the boss is and girlfriend, that be you!"

Cleopatra's New Attitude

"Stop killing the King's English and get you little narrow ass out of my office before I throw something at you," chuckled Cleopatra.

Poopie took his time and strolled casually out of the office grinning and shaking his head. He had become a good and faithful friend to Cleopatra. Had it not been for him, Cleo probably would have lost it a few times. He was always there to pick up the slack at work for her and he never disappointed her when she just needed someone to talk to. It had surprised her immensely that she had become so attached to a gay man. But, if the truth had to be told, he had proven to be one of the best friends any girl could have. Gay men and women just seemed to gel and understand each other's problems and Cleo was very glad Poopie had become her friend.

Keeping herself busy meeting with clients and returning phone calls, Cleopatra did not realize it was past 5 o'clock. *Goodness*, she thought, *how did the time fly by so quickly? I need to hurry and get out of here so I can meet Leonard as promised. I wonder just what kind of surprise he has for me today. I can't wait to see him.*

"See you later Cleopatra, I'm on my way out the door," shouted Poopie as he locked his desk drawer and put his computer to bed for the evening.

"Wait for me Poopie. I can't stay here a minute longer because I'm suppose to meet someone this evening."

Turning to see his friend rushing to get out of the office Poopie knew that whoever the friend was had to be somebody special. He had never seen her so animated and the smile on her face said she was really happy. His first thought was to question her about the "friend" she was rushing to meet, but his second thought was that if whoever this friend was could put that kind of smile on her face, they were alright in his book. All he ever wanted for Cleopatra was for her to be happy and she seemed to be glowing with happiness.

CHAPTER 30

"Oh me, oh my . . . ."

Arriving at her house, Cleo spotted Leonard in her front yard pulling weeds from her flowers around the mailbox and started chuckling at the sight. He seemed thoroughly engrossed in his task by pulling a weed and taking a good look at the dirt around the flowers.

What in the world is he looking for? she thought, *He's on his hands and knees and looking as if he's found something interesting among the flowers. I wish I had a camera to take a picture of this, nobody would believe that metro-man Leonard Wilkins is digging in somebody's flowers and pulling weeds.*

Looking up just as Cleo pulled into the driveway, Leonard rose from his task and walked to the car to open the door for her. "Don't say anything, I know you're wondering what I'm looking for in that little area of flowers. I have the same flowers planted near my patio in the backyard and I had a recent problem with aphids. It seems your flowers are suffering from the same little varmints. If you don't mind, I will ask my gardener to come by and spray for you. He can also do a little landscaping for you around the house and give you some flowers that will bloom continually during the summer months."

Mercedes M. Alexander

"You would do that for me? Did I really hear you say you had a gardener?"

"Yes, I really have a gardener and for you I would do anything, all you have to do is ask."

Grabbing his hand and pulling him toward the front door, Cleo turned and gave him a peck on the cheek. "Be careful with your promises, I just might expect you to follow through."

"I don't think you fully understand my intentions Ms. Beavers, I intend to be your everything, your best friend, lover, confidant, provider, sugar daddy and hopefully one day your husband."

"Whoa, slow your roll Leonard. Did I hear you say one day you hope to be my husband? Whatever happened to that ladies man who was more than happy being single and able to do whatever he pleased?"

Grabbing Cleo around the waist and starring into her eyes, Leonard studied her face carefully before he spoke. "That man found God, then, he found you Cleo. That man now realizes he wasn't put on this earth to live alone and he has promised God if he would bless him with you in his life, he would walk the straight and narrow and serve him as he should for the rest of his life. I haven't always been husband material and I have made so many mistakes in my life but, I'm here now willing and ready to make a drastic change and promise you that I will never make you unhappy."

With tears running down her cheek, Cleo could only nod her head in approval. "That was beautiful Leonard. I know God always answers prayers, but I want to take this one step at a time. I feel so alive when I'm with you and you make me happy. I need time to get myself together and I need to have a serious talk with you about children."

Cleopatra's New Attitude

"Ok, we'll take our time and the subject of children is something I want to discuss with you too. For now, run upstairs and put on something comfortable, I'm taking you to my house and serving dinner. I slaved in the kitchen for two hours this afternoon and all I need to do is put our steaks on the grill."

Running up the stairs to get changed, Cleo could not believe her ears, the man actually cooks. He was quickly becoming her dream man, good in bed and could rock her world, cooks and promises to do everything in his power to always make her happy. *God, please let him be the one*, she silently prayed, *I need someone in my life to make me happy and I want a family.*

*   *   *

Leonard drove quickly through the city to the other side of town. He was now passing open fields and newly developed housing areas. When he finally turned into a beautiful gated community, Cleo's eyes scanned the area and noticed the large homes on at least two acres of land and beautiful landscaped yards. The car soon pulled into a two-story home that was nothing short of a mansion.

"Is this where you live Leonard?" she asked as she turned her head from side to side trying to take in the area."

Reaching for Cleopatra's hand and staring into her eyes Leonard spoke quietly with a serious look on his face. "Yes, it's where I live, but it's not the type of home I want it to be. There's one missing ingredient and as soon as that is added this house will be complete and considered my home."

Turning to look at Leonard, Cleopatra took his hand and gave it a squeeze. "You could have just about any woman in Memphis. Why did you choose me and do you really feel you could be happy with me."

"Let's get in the house and discuss that little issue later. Believe it or not, I never thought I would ever fall for any woman as I have for you. But here I am, head over heels in love with you and enjoying every minute of it."

Walking into the house, Cleo was amazed at how tastefully it was decorated. It was basically decorated with brown and gold tones and occasionally there would be a splash of orange, red or yellow presented in the form of flowers, art fixtures, pillows or other interesting items that had been placed around the house. The furniture was masculine and large, dark wood blinds were the only covering for the massive windows in the house.

"While I'm getting the grill ready and checking on the other food, make yourself at home and roam around the house. If you don't want to take the stairs to go up, there's an elevator behind the first door in the hallway. Make sure you're out on the deck in the next thirty minutes. Just walk through the living room and go through the double doors leading to the library. The deck is just outside the double doors at the back of the library."

Feeling like a kid in a toy store, Cleopatra was already heading up the stairs and blowing kisses at Leonard.

*   *   *

The entire house was absolutely gorgeous. There were four bedrooms upstairs, each with its own private bath, a sitting room with a plasma T.V.

Cleopatra's New Attitude

on the wall and a private theatre with fancy seats and a full bar. Cleopatra found the elevator and stepped into it to go downstairs. On the first level she found a huge master bedroom. The California King bed had a bed cover with pillows on it that looked as if it should have been on the cover of a Neiman Marcus catalog. The master bath was larger than any she had ever seen and there was a separate powder room leading to the bath. The whirlpool bathtub was sitting in the middle of the room. It had been built-up at least two feet from the floor with marble steps leading to the tub. There were beautiful multi-colored candles of different shapes and sizes placed around the bath and each sat on different but coordinated gold candle holders. There were three doors in the bathroom. One opened to a private toilet and bidet and the other two led to private his and her closets. One closet held Leonard's clothes and was organized by shirts, pants, suits, shoes and jackets. The other closet was completely empty! In one corner of the bath was a glass enclosed shower that was large enough for four people and had a Grecian carving in the center on the wall with a coordinating bench that was L-shaped around two walls of the shower.

My goodness, thought Cleo, *I knew Leonard was doing well but I never imagined he was doing this well*. She came out of the bath and noticed a small hallway under the stairs that led to another part of the house. Making her way down the hall she came upon another bedroom. This one had a sitting room, a large bedroom and a bath that was done in pink marble. It was just as beautiful as the master bath but not as large.

The living room, first floor den, dining room and kitchen were equally impressive. Walking out onto the large deck, Cleo saw a sunroom she had not noticed that had to be connected to the master bedroom. The deck had furniture that was comfortable and it was clear somebody had taken

Mercedes M. Alexander

a lot of time strategically placing the furniture so that the area was an eye catcher. This was the first deck Cleo had ever seen that had matching cocktail tables, lamps and centerpieces placed in different areas. When she turned she saw a large wall water fountain with a lion's head. Water was spewing from the lion's mouth into a two tiered fountain. Leonard was busy cooking the steaks on his fancy grill under an area that had been specially built for him.

"Well, you decided to join me. Your steak will be ready in another two or three minutes and we can dine inside or out, it's your choice."

"Leonard, this house is a dream, I can't believe you live in such luxury. I know you have someone to come and clean because everything is in its place and the house looks as if it's ready for you to entertain at anytime. Are you really that neat and organized or does someone come in periodically and clean?"

"I'm pretty neat and I'll pick up after myself but, the cleaning is done by a service company. All this house needs now is you Cleopatra." Leonard was talking while peeping over the grill. Cleopatra could not see the mysterious grin he had on his face but she could hear the mischievousness in his voice.

The dinner was great. Leonard proved that he knew his way around the grill and the kitchen. After dinner they sat on the deck sipping wine and enjoying the breeze. They were sitting in a large recliner made for two that rocked them slowly back and forth. Cleopatra was getting a buzz from the wine and everything was right with the world. Leonard was keenly aware of her sitting so close to him in the recliner and kept his hands to himself as long as he could. He finally reached over and pulled her to him. They kissed and teased each other for over an hour until they

Cleopatra's New Attitude

could no longer stand it and headed inside the house. Unknown to them, there was someone watching the entire scenario and she was very unhappy about what she was seeing.

Leonard led Cleopatra to the first floor master bedroom suite. He slowly undressed her and kissed her body inch by inch as he slid her clothing from her pulsating body. After only five minutes of teasing her and feeling her body tense under his touch, he could no longer contain himself and stripped as quickly as possible. The lovemaking was entirely different from their experiences on the yacht. This was more intense and felt familiar and comfortable. Their bodies related to each other as if they were one once they were conjoined in the heat of their passion. Cleopatra never thought Leonard could take her any higher on the pleasure scale than he had on their little trip but, tonight he took her orgasms to higher and higher heights, she thought she was losing her mind as she was writhing under his lovemaking and finally screamed with pleasure.

"Oh baby," moaned Leonard, "I've never felt this way before. I'm so weak for you Cleopatra and I love you more than I ever thought I could love any woman. I need you in my life and I want to wake up each morning with you beside me. Please let me prove to you over and over again for the rest of my life how much I love you."

As Leonard took Cleopatra again and again all she could do was shiver and say, "Yes".

Outside lurking in the dark around Leonard's car was Rachel Bennett. She was not very happy with the scene she saw on the deck as she used the telescope from her bedroom to spy on Leonard. After watching Leonard and Cleo kissing and holding each other so passionately on the deck, she knew exactly what they were doing in the house and she was boiling inside

Mercedes M. Alexander

with anger. Taking a small steak knife from her pocket, Rachel punctured two of Leonard's tires. Feeling a little vindicated after ruining the tires, Rachel made up her mind to find out just who the little bitch was and make her life miserable.

CHAPTER 31

"And I'm telling you, I'm not going . . . ."

"Leonard, honey, wake up. It's almost midnight and we both have to work tomorrow."

Turning slowly with a huge smile on his face, Leonard was wishing they didn't have to part. He felt so damn comfortable with this woman and she was just where she needed to be, in his home, in his bed and in his arms.

"I'm not asleep Cleopatra and I love it when you call me "honey." That's what my grandmother called my grandfather and she always had a special ring in her voice when she called him that. I distinctly heard that same ring in your voice and it warmed me from my head to my feet. Please stay and I promise to take you home early in the morning so you'll have time to get dressed for work."

"Alright, you've twisted my arm. I'll stay with you tonight on one condition."

Just as Leonard was going to ask what her condition was the phone rang. He reached over and answered it. After a limited conversation, he hung up with an uneasy look on his face.

Mercedes M. Alexander

Sensing that something was wrong, Cleopatra reached out to him. "What's up Leonard, what was that phone call about?

"Stay here while I check something outside. That call was from my neighbor across the street. He said he saw someone outside on my driveway hiding behind the car. I need to check this out and I want you to stay put."

As Leonard walked outside to check around the front of the house, he immediately noticed the tires on his Jag. His first thought went to Rachel, he knew in his gut she was the culprit. Walking back inside the house, he made up his mind to call the police and have them fill out a report and investigate the vandalism. He could smell trouble on the horizon; Rachel would prove to be a problem.

* * *

Strolling casually into her office the next morning, Cleopatra was all smiles. She felt like a woman who had just hit the jackpot. She was in love with a man who treated her like a queen and had confessed his love to her, she had the job of her dreams and all was right with the world. As she flipped through her calendar to check her schedule for the week Poopie popped his head in her door.

"Alright sweetie, just where were you last night? I called your house several times and decided to give up at eleven thirty and turn in for the night."

Smiling from ear to ear, Cleo could not contain her joy. She was about to burst with her happiness and needed to tell someone just how she felt. Beckoning for her friend to sit, she stepped toward the door to close it so they could have some privacy.

Cleopatra's New Attitude

"Poopie, you would not believe just what has happened in my life in the last few weeks. I have never been so happy and I keep wanting to pinch myself to make sure I'm not dreaming. My relationship with Leonard has moved up a few levels, I know I'm in love with him. He says that he loves me too and has just about promised me the world and wants me to be his wife. Of course I intend to wait awhile before I announce any of this to my parents or my girlfriends because it's only been a short time since Robert's death and I know I need to appear as if I'm grieving."

Snapping his fingers and weaving his head Poopie was laughing at Cleo's revelation. "Hold it, hold it girlfriend. First let me say that I'm happy for you and then let me say that you shouldn't give a damn what anybody thinks about your relationship or how fast you're moving with it. Nobody went through all that bullshit with Robert and his whoremonger behind but you, so don't think twice about whatever a few tongue wagging, jealous bitches think. Now I know you love your girls but don't think there won't be any jealousy involved if you proclaim all this happiness to them. Women are natural bitches and cannot help feeling jealousy. Anyway, after they digest it all and sit down to think they'll be cool about it. I know they love you and will stand with you. And all the other people out there can just go to hell."

"Thanks Poopie, I knew you would understand. I tried to take it slow but my heart and body wouldn't listen. My girlfriends aren't bitches, they really care about me and will go after any man if he really hurt me."

Cleo continued telling Poopie all the details of her trip and even told of how she and the Golden Girls had tried to put Leonard in his place. All the while, Poopie sat silently listening and smiling while nodding his head in approval. Whoever said that a gay man could be a woman's best friend

Mercedes M. Alexander

had never lied; Poopie was turning out to be someone Cleopatra could confide in and rely on. She knew her secrets were safe with him.

*   *   *

Leonard had made a special detour after dropping Cleopatra at her house that morning. He went straight to the offices of the private detective he had hired to keep a watchful eye on Cleo. He had decided during the night that he would know Rachel's every move. He could not afford having her interfere with his relationship with Cleopatra. He was also worried that if she had the nerve to slash his tires, she could possibly do harm to Cleopatra. *God,* he thought, *what in the hell was I thinking when I let that woman in my bed.*

Two hours later while sitting in his office Leonard sat smiling to himself about his evening with Cleopatra. His secretary interrupted his thoughts by buzzing him to say that there was an irate woman in the outer office demanding to see him. Stepping out to the waiting room of his office, Leonard saw Rachel standing with her hands on her hips and staring out the window. His first thought was to turn and walk back to his office, lock the door and just ignore her. However, he knew he needed to end any of Rachel's thoughts about them ever being a couple. He also needed to let her know there was another woman in his life and he was serious about her.

"Hello Rachael, what brings you to my office today? It's been a while since I've seen you."

When Rachel turned around Robert was startled at how wretched she looked. She had been crying and her eyes were red and swollen.

Cleopatra's New Attitude

"Don't start any small talk with me Leonard. You know exactly why I'm here. I had two police officers knocking on my door this morning questioning me about slicing the tires on your car last night. I lied and told them I didn't do it but after thinking about it I decided to confess to you that I did it and I would do it again. I saw you with that hussy last night and if I could have gotten my hands on her, I would have slit her throat instead of your tires."

"Step into my office Rachel. I think we need to do some serious talking about what you did. I'm not going to press charges against you but we need to get a few things straight."

Ushering Rachel into his office, Leonard told the secretary to hold all his calls. He knew this would take a while because the one thing he knew about Rachel was that she would not give up or give in without a fight. He had to make her accept the fact that she would never be the woman in his life.

"Sit here on the sofa Rachel. Can I get you any coffee or some other type of beverage?"

"Cut the crap Leonard, my reason for coming here was not just to confess that I slit your tires, I also want you to know that I don't have any intentions of letting some other woman get her claws into you without a fight. I have waited too long to have you and will not stand idly by while some twit waltzes into your house and takes what I want for myself."

"Whoa Rachel, I'm not something up for grabs for you or any woman. If I led you on in the past, I apologize for that. The night we spent together was a mistake and I have regretted it ever since. Nobody is waltzing into my home or my life. I happen to have pursued a woman who I deeply love and who I want to spend the rest of my life making happy. I'm sorry if you

Mercedes M. Alexander

thought there was something in the cards for the two of us but that was never my intention."

Out of nowhere, Rachel jumped up and started scratching at Leonard. It took everything he had not to knock the woman to her senses. Trying to hold her still and keep her from injuring him was proving to be quite a task. Rachel was stronger than she looked and Leonard was starting to think he just might have to hit her to stop her attack. After a few minutes of tussling with her, Rachel fell to the floor sobbing.

"I love you Leonard, I can't live without you and I won't. I want to know who this bitch is and I can guarantee you when I finish with her, she will not cross your path again. Whether you believe it or not, you belong to me and I'm not having it any other way."

Standing to her feet, Rachel straighten her clothes and walked swiftly out the office door with the strangest look on her face. Leonard knew he had to warn Cleopatra about the woman. His only fear was that Cleopatra would not understand and asked for details about his relationship with the new raving lunatic in his life.

Picking up the receiver on the phone, Leonard took a deep breath and asked his secretary to call the hotel and have him connected to Cleopatra.

"Hi Babe, it's me. How has your morning been thus far?"

"Oh hi honey, it's been absolutely perfect. How has your morning been?"

"That's what I'm calling about Cleopatra. I don't want to talk about this on the phone. Can we meet after work and have a quiet dinner? I know a nice restaurant near Germantown I think you'll like. Can I pick you up at seven?"

Cleopatra's New Attitude

"Sure you can Leonard. I'll be waiting"

Hanging up the phone on her end, Cleopatra felt goose bumps rising on her arms. Something was not quite right and Leonard sounded much too serious about needing to talk with her.

CHAPTER 32

"Your blessing is coming . . . ."

Trying to work through the evening and wrap things up for the day proved to be a tremendous task for Cleopatra. Right in the middle of the afternoon Elaine Williams appeared in her office with little Alexis on her hip. The child was dressed in pink with little pigtails on each side of her head. Cleo couldn't help but think that the child looked adorable clinging to her grandmother.

"Hello Mrs. Williams, this is quite a surprise. What brings you and little Alexis to my office today?"

Walking as if it took a lot of effort, Mrs. Williams sat in the nearest chair and looked as if she would faint. Cleo reached for the child to take the burden from the older woman and called Poopie to bring water. After Mrs. Williams had caught her breath and seemed a little more relaxed, Poopie took little Alexis down to the gift shop to buy her a lollipop so the two women could talk.

"Forgive me for barging in on you this way. I just left my doctor's office and had my neighbor to drop me off at your office. She's outside waiting in the lobby area of the hotel. I wanted you to know that Paula

Mercedes M. Alexander

has gotten married and doesn't want her new husband to know about the child. She has signed all parental rights over to me. I'm an old woman Mrs. Beavers and I can't raise a child. The Lord could call me any day and where would that leave my darling Alexis. My arthritis acts up daily and I don't have the energy to run behind an active little girl. It breaks my heart to think that something could happen to me and that little girl could end up in foster care."

"Oh Mrs. Williams, don't be so gloomy," exclaimed Cleo while she patted the older woman's hand. "What makes you think you're ready to leave this earth? That child just might be what you need to keep you active and give you a reason to live."

"No baby, that's not going to happen, I know what I'm saying and I need to make sure that child is provided for. Now I appreciate the checks you've been sending since her daddy passed away but I need something else from you. I need you to promise you will take Alexis and raise her if something happens to me. You're a young woman and the child seems to take to you. I know this is asking a lot but I don't have anyone else to turn to and you seem to be the logical person since you are her stepmother."

Cleo slumped back into her chair with her mind racing. She had never thought of herself as the little girl's stepmother.

"Look Mrs. Williams, this will take some time to sink in. I won't say that I wouldn't take Alexis and raise her if something happened to you but there are other things I have to consider before I make a commitment like that."

"Take all the time you need child, just keep in mind my time may not be long. I just wanted to put it on your mind right now just in case something should happen to me. I'll take my leave now. Where did that man take little Alexis?"

Cleopatra's New Attitude

"Oh, he's not far. Let me help you up and I'll find them for you."

Cleopatra found Poopie and Alexis in the restaurant looking at the fish in the large aquarium. She took the child to her grandmother and watched as they left the building.

Standing in her office doorway with his hands on his hips, Poopie was looking puzzled and seemed to be waiting for an explanation about the older woman and the child. After Cleo offered no explanation, Poopie could no longer contain himself and switched over to the desk, placed both hands on it and stared Cleo in the eyes.

"Ok girlfriend, what's up with that?" I know when something strange is going on with you and I had a tingling up my spine when I saw you holding that little girl."

Knowing the cat would be out of the bag soon enough, Cleo decided to tell Poopie all about Michael's love child.

"Poopie, that little girl is Michael's and that was her grandmother. The mother is gone and wants nothing to do with the child and now the grandmother wants me to raise her. The little girl is precious and well behaved. I have this feeling of fullness in my chest every time I see her and I'm content when I hold her in my arms. I know this sounds crazy, but I want that child. Not because she's Michael's but simply because she needs me and this may be the only way I will ever have a child of my own."

As Poopie looked down at Cleo, he saw tears well up in her eyes and knew that she would do the right thing when it came to raising the little girl. His first thought was that Cleo was a natural with the child and they looked like a mother and daughter duo.

"Cleopatra, don't you dare start crying in this office. You know how emotional I am and if you cry, I'll start crying and this office will be a mess. If I were in your shoes, I'd take little Alexis and raise her. She looks like she could be yours and I know you would make a wonderful mother. Look at it this way—yes, Michael was a bastard but he couldn't have left a more beautiful child on this earth. It's almost karma, maybe this child is here to give you a chance to be a mother and to forgive Michael. Just thank him for this precious gift and drop the hatred, you can then move on with your life and make a home for that little girl."

"Thanks Poopie, I needed to hear that. To be honest with you, I have fallen in love with that little girl. Whenever I hold her, her presence pulls my heart strings and makes me smile. I just wonder what Leonard will say and if he'll think I'm crazy for wanting to raise Michael's child."

She knew in her heart that she wouldn't hesitate to raise the child, but what would Leonard think and how would it affect their relationship? She knew not too many men would want to take on a woman and a child that was not his. Although she knew Leonard loved children, she was not sure just how far that love would go if he had to take one on a permanent basis. Well, Leonard had something important he wanted to tell her and now she had a bombshell she needed to drop on him.

*   *   *

At precisely 6:55 p.m., Leonard was at Cleopatra's door. He was dressed casually and had a dozen yellow roses in his arms. Just seeing him made Cleopatra light up. The man could work his magic on her without even trying; she was falling deeply in love with him.

"Ready to go? I'm starved and I hope you have an appetite. This restaurant has the best lobster in the area and it's an all you can eat menu."

Cleopatra's New Attitude

"Yes, I'm ready. Let me grab my purse and we can leave."

Looking at Cleopatra made Leonard smile. He seemed to be smiling a lot lately and the world seemed to be a brighter place. He had the distinct feeling this evening would prove to be interesting. His only hope was that Cleopatra would hear him out and know that he was telling her the truth about his relationship with Rachel for two reasons. The first reason being that he needed her to know Rachel could be dangerous and the second reason was that he had to tell her he never had feelings for the woman and only had one sexual encounter with the nut case.

Entering the restaurant, Cleopatra gave Leonard's hand a squeeze. He smelled so good, his hands were perfectly manicured, his freshly shaved face seemed ruggedly handsome and she loved his suave way of walking. Any fool in the place could look at her and tell she was smitten with the man. She suddenly realized she had never been in love before she met Leonard. She had wasted a lot of time and years while living with Robert and thinking she loved him. Now she had a new attitude about love and she knew what love really felt like, she could not imagine how she existed without it for so long. She needed to get in her mind how she would address the issue of raising Alexis with Leonard. This was much too important to put off and it had to be discussed tonight.

The waiter quickly seated Cleopatra and Leonard after they entered the restaurant. The place was quite elegant for a seafood buffet. Cleopatra thought it was amusing for the place to be so elaborate and then let it's guest fend for themselves hovering over an open buffet. The waiter offered them menus just in case they decided not to have the buffet. When Cleo saw the prices listed for entrees from the menu and the price of the buffet, she knew that this was a five star restaurant. The prices were exorbitant!

Mercedes M. Alexander

"Come back to me Cleopatra", exclaimed Leonard as he snapped his fingers in front of Cleo. "You look as if you're in a trance. Did the prices on the menu shock you or do you have some deep secret on your mind."

Reaching across the table, Cleopatra took Leonard's hand and squeezed it very lovingly. She looked into his eyes and began to tell him how much he meant to her and how happy she was that he had come into her life. Sensing that something was troubling Cleopatra and that it was about to be expressed by her, Robert quickly started to tell her how he loved her and reiterated that he would do anything in the world to make her happy and keep her by his side.

"Cleo, wait a minute, you look tense and now I'm getting worried about whatever it is that brought up this conversation. I should be the one to start the conversation since I invited you to dinner to discuss something important with you. Let me get this off my chest first baby then you can tell me whatever you feel you need to tell. The waiter is coming over again so let's just order from the menu and that will give us some time to talk before our dinner arrives."

They both ordered the salmon dish the restaurant was famous for and quickly picked up on their conversation.

Leonard cleared his throat and began first. "Do you remember when we were on the yacht and I tried to tell you a little of my history with other women and said that lately I have had only one indiscretion?

Cleo nodded her head.

"There is this woman I've known for a long time. In fact, she was a friend of my ex-wife and as soon as my wife left the scene, this woman started trying to be my best friend. I knew she had ulterior motives and I had been very good at keeping her at arm's length. Believe me when I

Cleopatra's New Attitude

say that I had no romantic inclinations toward her and never touched her. After you decided you wanted space between us because of that first kiss, I was at a very low point in my life. Rachel connived her way into my home one evening while carrying her own bottle of champagne. I drank a little too much and ended up in bed with her. I felt so bad about it the next morning and I took extra effort not to be involved with her again. I made sure that we didn't see each other and kept making excuses whenever she called. Well, she decided to pop-up again and she was the one to slash my tires when you were with me last night. She arrived at my office this morning threatening to do whatever she has to do to have me for her own. I'm really worried that the fool might actually go after you. I've taken extra precautions for your safety. I hired a private investigator to follow her and keep an eye on her for a while. I don't want you to be in any type of danger on account of me. The lunatic actually tried to attack me today in my office."

Moving her chair around the table to be closer to Leonard, Cleopatra actually smiled at him, then she chuckled.

"Don't think I'm going to tuck tail and run because some dizzy broad wants my man. I'm a big girl and I can handle myself Leonard. If she thinks she can bully me, she has another thought coming and it won't be a pleasant one. If that's what you're so worried about you can put your mind at ease. I'm not easily frightened and if she approaches me, at least I have heads up on what to expect. Thank you for telling me honey, you don't know how much I appreciate your honesty, that honesty alone lets me know that I can trust you."

Breathing a sigh of relief, Leonard leaned over and kissed Cleo on her cheek. He felt as if a huge weight had been lifted from his shoulders.

Mercedes M. Alexander

"Now that you have told me your concern, I have something I need to tell you," exclaimed Cleo. "During all of Robert's whoring around he made the mistake of fathering a child. The little girl's name is Alexis and she's about two years old. She's the most beautiful child and is being raised by an elderly great-grandmother. The mother has married and moved on with her life and does not want the child. She's signed all parental rights over to the great-grandmother and Alexis will probably never see her mother again. Mrs. Williams visited me at my office today and asked me if I would take the child and raise her as my own. I'm still reeling from my conversation with her and I wanted to ask you what it would do to our relationship if there was a child in the picture."

Laughing uncontrollably, Leonard kept shaking his head trying to regain his composure. He reached over again and kissed Cleopatra very lightly on her lips, this time with possessiveness he had never displayed before. "Oh baby, I love children. I have been mentoring a young boy in my church. Matthew is six years old and quite the little man. I want you to meet him and maybe you can bring Alexis along and the four of us can do something together. It is ironic that you've been asked to take Alexis as your own, I've been approached about taking Matthew and raising him. Your father had a large role in my meeting Matthew and he has been gently pushing me to take total responsibility for the child."

The waiter appeared at the table with their dinner. Not noticing anything the waiter did, the two lovers just sat there and smiled at each other.

After their dinner on the drive home Cleopatra wanted to know as much about Matthew as Leonard could tell her. "Wouldn't we make the perfect family Leonard? Alexis would have a big brother and two children would have a mother and a father. Your house is perfect for raising two children and the schools near your home are suppose to be the best in the district. I can't believe how God is smiling on us. It seems like a fairy tale but I think I'll call it a blessed tale, because we have four people involved in a unique situation that can be called nothing but a blessing."

Cleopatra starting humming to the music playing on the radio. The song being played was one by a popular gospel choir, "The Struggle is Over For You" were the words to the song. Cleo felt as if God had ordained that song to be played just for her. "Leonard, since we're talking about children and a life together, don't you think we need to talk to my parents? They will be surprised enough when we tell them about us and it will completely blow them over when we talk about the children—their future grandkids."

"Yes, we do need to talk with your parents. We also need to let Mr. and Mrs. Beavers know that they have a grandchild. It may be of some comfort to them to know that a part of their son still lives on in Alexis."

"Oh my God, I never thought about that, how callous of me to not tell them about their grandchild. I can't believe I didn't think to tell them about Alexis. I know they will be thrilled to have a granddaughter. It's still early Leonard, I know my parents are up and about. Can we go by their house now and tell them about us? I want to wait a week or so before we tell them about the children. I think a little information at a time is all they can digest."

"Sure we can, I would like to tell your father man-to-man tonight that I love his daughter and I would like for him and your mother to give us their blessing."

"Ok, do you mean their blessing for us to be a couple or their blessing for marriage?

Mercedes M. Alexander

Thinking about what she had just said Leonard realized that he wanted to ask for her hand in marriage right then and there. Pulling his car over to the side near the river park, he ran to the other side of the car and opened Cleopatra's door. He led her to one of the park benches and while sitting under the moonlight, Leonard dropped to one knee and asked her to marry him.

"Cleopatra, I prayed for God to send you to me, I pray for you more than I pray for myself. When I'm not with you, my mind wanders to thoughts of you constantly. I can close my eyes and smell your scent, feel your touch and hear your voice. I love you baby and I want you in my life forever. Will you marry me Cleopatra and be a mother to Alexis and Matthew?

With tears streaming down her face Cleopatra could only whisper, "Yes, I'll marry you Leonard and be a mother to our children who have been directed to us by God."

Leonard was more than happy to hear Cleopatra say yes and to discuss the children as if they were already a family. *A family*, he thought. *I can't thank God enough for this opportunity to have Cleo willing to be my wife and two children to complete our lives.*

CHAPTER 33

"What God has for me is for me . . . ."

Reverend and Mrs. Handy were ecstatic to learn that Leonard and Cleopatra considered themselves a couple. However, they were completely shocked to learn that Leonard had proposed to Cleo and that she had accepted.

Mrs. Handy was the first to speak, "Well child, I know you had a lot of trials in your last relationship and I've secretly known that you were not happy with Michael. There was never a light in your eyes when you were with him. You just seemed to go through life living day by day and doing what needed to be done to survive."

"What do you mean when you say you knew I wasn't happy with Michael? Did I do or say anything that made me seem unhappy?"

Going over to sit with Cleopatra, Mrs. Handy put her arms around her only daughter's shoulders. "Cleo, a woman has joy on her face when she calls her husband's name, she smiles when he touches her and lingers close to him when in public places. I never saw any of that when you were with Michael. However, I did see signs of it the day your father and I walked into your house before Michael's funeral and saw you with Leonard."

Mercedes M. Alexander

Cleopatra was shocked and a little embarrassed. "Mother, was it so obvious then? I can't believe that I was that transparent."

Rev. Handy walked over to Leonard and winked. He had such a mischievous look on his face and chuckled as he talked. "Child, your mother told me when we left your house that day you had the look of love on your face. My only comment was that you could not have found a better man. I think the world of Leonard and yes, you two have our blessing and I know you'll be happy together."

"Let's break out the champagne," Mrs. Handy announced. "I have a bottle in the fridge that is long overdue for a celebration."

The four of them toasted the happy occasion and talked for hours about family, plans for the future and how happy they were about Leonard joining the family.

*   *   *

One week later Cleopatra picked up little Alexis and met Leonard and Matthew at the park. Leonard explained to Matthew that he and Cleo would be getting married in the near future and if he wanted to be their son, they would be happy to be his new mom and dad. Matthew was beside himself jumping up and down. He was then told Alexis would be his little sister and they would all live in Leonard's house. The children got along beautifully and Matthew was already playing the role of big brother by pushing Alexis on the swing while telling the other children he was taking care of his little sister.

Oh God, please let this not be a dream, thought Cleopatra as she watched the children play. It was all too good to be true. She was here with the

Cleopatra's New Attitude

man of her dreams watching her children, children she never thought she would have. It seemed as if life had done a full circle for her and she was now being blessed with all God had promised.

"Ok kids, we have to leave now. We have one more stop to make before we go to dinner and we need to get moving." Leonard was waving for the children to come to them as they readied to leave the park.

Cleo grabbed Matthew's hand and Leonard put Alexis on his shoulders. Anyone watching the foursome would think they were the perfect family.

The next stop would be the home of Mr. and Mrs. Beavers. Cleopatra had made up her mind she would go by their house today to introduce Alexis to her grandparents and to announce her plans to marry Leonard. She knew they would be overjoyed about meeting their grandchild but the news of her upcoming marriage may not go over as well.

*   *   *

Cleopatra stood at the door of her former in-laws with Alexis in her arms and rung the doorbell. The child had gone to sleep in the car and was still sleeping peacefully after she had been lifted from the car. Leonard stood behind Cleopatra holding Matthew's hand.

Mrs. Beavers opened the door. "Goodness gracious, look who's come to visit." She ushered Cleo and her little group into the living room and called upstairs for Mr. Beavers to come and greet their guest.

Mr. Beavers gave Cleopatra a hug and shook Leonard's hand. He reached for Matthew's little hand and told Cleo and Leonard that he was a fine looking little boy.

Mercedes M. Alexander

Sitting on the sofa with Alexis in her lap Cleopatra cleared her throat and patted the sofa for Leonard and Matthew to sit beside her.

"This is Leonard Wilkins and little Matthew. We decided to come by this evening so you could meet somebody. I know I haven't talked with you very often since Michael's death but I had some issues I had to deal with for myself. I have now gotten my life together and I wanted you to see the child Michael fathered. This little girl is Michael's child and her name is Alexis."

Mrs. Beavers looked as if she would faint and leaned against her husband. Both of the elder Beavers had a look of shock on their faces. Mrs. Beavers slowly reached for Alexis and Cleopatra handed the sleeping child to her. Michael's parents sat and stared at the little girl as if she was sent from heaven.

With tears flowing from her eyes, Mrs. Beavers started thanking the Lord for letting them live to see a grandchild that was of their own flesh. She rocked the child back and forth for a few minutes before she was able to talk. All the while, Mr. Beavers just smiled and gently patted Alexis' face.

"How long have you known about the baby Cleopatra and where is her mother? Where does she live? How old is she?" Questions starting popping out of the mouths of Jerry and John Beavers. They were amazed at the child and wanted to know everything about her.

Cleopatra gently told them when and how she found out about the child. She also explained the circumstances of Alexis' mother and great-grandmother and that she would be formally adopting the child when she and Leonard got married.

"Married? What do you mean by getting married? My boy has been dead for less than half a year and you're already talking about getting married again. Who is this man and just how long has this been going on?" Mrs. Beavers was full of questions and used an accusing tone as she asked them.

Leonard looked at Cleo and sighed deeply while Cleopatra sat and shook her head. She knew this news would be a shocker to the Beavers but Cleopatra did not expect such a negative reaction. Standing to walk over to Mrs. Beavers, Cleopatra looked back at Leonard with regret in her eyes. Why did she pounce on the elderly couple with so much information at one time? She should have given them only the information about their grandchild and waited until another time to explain her upcoming marriage to Leonard.

"Mother Beavers, please know that I never did anything wrong during my marriage to Michael. I was a faithful wife and did everything in my power to make sure that he was happy. However, he had other ideas and I cannot count the women he fooled around with while he was married to me. This child is positive proof that he was not faithful to me and if you want to hear the whole sordid truth about all the other women I will be more than happy to relate the entire story to you. However, I don't think this is the time or place. Please give Alexis back to me and Leonard and I will take our leave."

Slowly handing the child back to Cleopatra, Mr. Beavers broke down in tears and started to apologize to his wife. Mr. Beavers knew all about Michael's other women and had had long conversations with him about them. Michael had been encouraged by his father to mess around with as many women as he could. According to Mr. Beavers, he had told Michael that variety was the spice of life and his son had followed his path of being unfaithful to his wife. He blamed himself for Michael's death and could not control his agony as he fell to his knees sobbing.

Mercedes M. Alexander

"Please forgive me Jerry; I hate myself for what I did to our son and what I have done to you. It's all my fault that Michael died. If I had been a decent father, told him to be faithful to his wife, and not bragged about my conquests with other women, he probably would have been alive now. I failed him miserably and I failed you."

Jerry Beavers stood speechless as the blood drained from her face leaving her pale and ghostly looking. She walked over to her husband and slapped him as hard as she could then turned and walked up the stairs. They heard the door to the bedroom upstairs slam and lock. Not wanting to leave with the situation as tense as it was, Cleo handed Alexis to Leonard and asked him to sit with Mr. Beavers while she went upstairs to check on Jerry.

Knocking softly on the door to the bedroom, Cleopatra could hear Jerry softly crying. "Mother Beavers, please let me in. I am so sorry about all of this, but we need to talk. You don't have to carry this burden alone; I will always be your daughter-in-law and love you. Please, please open the door."

The door to the bedroom slowly opened and Jerry fell into Cleopatra's arms. Both of the women cried and Cleopatra prayed for a healing from God. As she prayed out loud, Jerry began to calm down and started whispering her own prayer. While sitting on the settee in the bedroom the two of them talked about forgiveness and what God would want them to do with their lives. Jerry Beavers said she did not know if she could offer forgiveness to her husband at this point but that she would not leave him and would work toward mending their marriage.

"Cleopatra, I'm an old woman and my husband would probably grieve himself to death if I left him. I know my faith in God will get me

Cleopatra's New Attitude

through this but I don't know if my husband will ever be able to forgive himself. I agree with him that he was my son's downfall. I always knew he was messing around and turned a blind eye to it. Over the years I have had women confront me in public places, make ugly phone calls and send anonymous letters. I was weak and kept it to myself instead of confronting it as a wife should. I'm just as guilty as John because I kept quiet. If only I had stood up to him and insisted that he walk the straight and narrow maybe John would have been a better example of what a husband should be and Michael would have been faithful to you."

"You can't blame yourself, Michael was a grown man and believe me he knew he was wrong. He may have used his father's example as an excuse to do his thing but nobody made him do anything. I think it's good that you will not leave your husband but I know it will be hard for you to trust him again and to be able to live with him. In times like these just put your trust in God, I know he will bring you through this. He never gives us a burden that we cannot bear, He has something in store for you, just sit still and wait on it."

"Cleopatra how can you stay so calm? How were you able to handle the knowledge about Michael's outside women without falling apart?"

While sitting, Cleo told Jerry Beavers her entire story because she felt she had nothing to hide. She told her how she met Leonard and how their relationship developed. She also told her that she never had any intentions of violating her marriage to Michael and never committed adultery or let Leonard get close enough to harm her marriage. After relating her feelings about Michael's indiscretions and the agony she went through Cleo lifted the older woman's face with her hands and looked her in her eyes.

Mercedes M. Alexander

"Please give me your blessing on my decision to marry Leonard. I don't want to have a strained relationship with you or John and I want the both of you in Alexis' life. You are her grandparents and she needs to know you and get to love you."

"Cleo, what I said earlier were words of a grieving mother and I spoke words that I now deeply regret. Of course I want you to be happy and you have my blessing. Thank you for being such a good wife to my son and nursing him through his illness. Thank you for always being so caring and trying to keep this family together. I love you as if you were my daughter and I always want to be a part of your life if you will allow me to be."

The two women hugged and cried again. There was a bond developed at that moment that would never be broken. Jerry Beavers had really gained a daughter and Cleopatra had gained another mother.

CHAPTER 34

"Oh happy day . . . ."

Cleopatra's parents were more than happy to learn of her intentions to adopt two beautiful children. They had long ago given up hope of ever being grandparents. Now they were doubly blessed with Matthew and Alexis. Because of the pending marriage, Cleo and Leonard both agreed they needed to belong to one church. Cleopatra would join her father's church and the two of them would get married there. Rev. Handy was overjoyed to have his daughter back in his flock and could not keep the tears from flowing when she walked down the aisle to join his membership. He would now have his daughter and her family with him every Sunday.

Cleopatra and Leonard spent every available waking moment with each other planning their future together. Life had never been better for either of them and the children made their lives even happier.

* * *

Six months later on Sunday morning, August 12th, there appeared in the Commercial Appeal society section a picture of Cleopatra and Leonard

Mercedes M. Alexander

announcing the engagement of the happy couple. Slowly reading the large write-up of the engaged couple and seething with anger was Rachel Bennett. During the last six or seven months she had been cordial with Leonard thinking he would come to his senses and realize that she was the woman for him. She did everything in her power to prove to him that she had changed and that he had made a mistake trying to push her out of his life. Although Leonard was always kind to her, he never did anything he thought would encourage the woman. Every time the woman approached him or called, Leonard made it a point to let Cleopatra know about the encounter and exactly what was said between the two of them.

Rachel was not a woman to be ignored. During her heyday, she was always the center of attention when she entered a room. In her mind, she still had the ability to demand the same attention from everybody—mostly men. Throwing the newspaper aside, Rachel quickly moved into action by getting dressed to the nines for church services. She had learned some time ago that Leonard had joined the Bethel Baptist Church in downtown Memphis. She would make her appearance there today to confront him and let him know that by no means would she accept him marrying another woman.

*   *   *

Leonard was promptly at Cleopatra's front door with Matthew in-tow at 10:15 a.m. as she had requested. Matthew was looking like a little man in the suit and shoes his parents—to—be had purchased for him the day before. He was quite proud of his grown-up attire and kept looking down

Cleopatra's New Attitude

at his new shoes with a grin on his face. Leonard was tickled at the look on Matt's face and the way he kept admiring himself.

Cleopatra answered the door on the second knock. She and Alexis had been ready for fifteen minutes and standing near the foyer waiting for Leonard to drive up. Alexis had on a yellow and white dress with lace and ruffles while her new mother had on the same colors. When Cleo and Alexis stepped out the front door anyone witnessing the scene would have said they were a good looking family.

"Hi Baby," exclaimed Leonard as he looked Cleopatra over. He could not take his eyes from her. Today was the day that everyone in the church and the city of Memphis would know she had promised to become his wife. Rev. Handy would also announce to the congregation that Leonard and Cleopatra were in the process of adopting Matthew and Alexis. This was going to be a wonderful day!

"Oh Leonard, you and Matthew look so handsome. Alexis and I are blessed to be escorted to church by the two of you."

"Daddy, do you like my dress?" was the first thing Alexis said in her little babyish voice.

Stooping down to pick her up, Leonard held her in the air and placed kisses all over her face. "I sure do sugar, you're the prettiest little girl in the whole world."

Grabbing Matthew's hand, Cleo lead the way to the car. Once Matthew had been buckled in and Alexis was placed in her car seat, the four of them headed out to church.

*　　*　　*

229

Mercedes M. Alexander

Bethel Baptist Church was overflowing with its members and visitors on this beautiful Sunday morning. Strutting in church like a proud peacock with a large ostentatious red and white hat, Rachel Bennett took a quick glance over the congregation looking for Leonard. There were so many people packed into the church that all she could see was a sea of heads and none of them looked like Leonard. She had to be content with taking a seat in the middle of the center aisle. She actually ignored the usher and marched up the aisle, forcing people in the pew to move over so she could sit on the end. Rev. Handy could not help but notice the brazen woman from his seat in the pulpit. His first thought was that she knew nothing about church etiquette and that he had never seen her before.

After the choir sang a few heartwarming selections, the clerk of the church stepped forward to read the announcements and welcome the visitors. As she read the names of each visitor, she asked that they stand so the congregation could see them. When she read Rachel Bennett's name, Leonard and Cleopatra looked behind them to see her standing to be recognized. Leonard immediately felt a knot forming in the pit of his stomach, he knew there would be trouble. Cleopatra sensing Leonard's uneasiness, reached for his hand and whispered that everything was going to be fine.

After the announcements, Rev. Handy stepped to the podium in the pulpit and ask for Cleopatra to come forward. Walking quickly over to the podium on the floor in front of the pulpit, Cleopatra stood and scanned the crowd with a smile on her face. As she cleared her throat, she looked directly at Rachel Bennett.

"I once read a book of quotes and one of the quotes by Nathaniel Parker Willis stood out in my mind as I thought of what I would say to you today. The quote is about love and it says, "If there is anything that

Cleopatra's New Attitude

keeps the mind open to angel visits, and repels the ministry of evil, it is pure human love." My love for the man in my life is pure and I know his love for me is pure."

Rachel Bennett bowed her head and could not look Cleopatra in the face. She sat in her seat and stared at the back of the pew in front of her. She felt a strange sensation when Cleopatra looked at her and made her quote of love and how it repels evil.

"I stand before you this morning to tell you of my love for God and how he has shown his love for me by sending a very special man to me. I would like for my fiancé Leonard Wilkins and my new son and daughter to come and stand with me. Daddy, would you be kind enough to finish the announcement?"

Leonard and the children joined Cleopatra at the front of the church, the children gathered around her with Alexis hugging her around her knees. Leonard put his arm around her waist and gave her a light kiss on the cheek.

Rev. Handy came from the pulpit and gave everybody a hug. He then made the announcement of the impending marriage and told everybody how happy he and his wife were, knowing they would have the chance to become grandparents. He then asked the congregation to bow their heads while he said a prayer to ask God to bless the family to be and to keep them in His care. A powerful prayer was given by Rev. Handy and when it was over not a dry eye was in the church. Even Rachel Bennett shed a few tears as she realized that Leonard was not in God's plan for her.

After the services, Cleopatra made a beeline for Rachel. Leonard looked around just as Cleo reached Rachel and put her hand on her shoulder. He stood peacefully to watch Cleopatra reach out to Rachel.

Mercedes M. Alexander

"Ms. Bennett, I want to formally introduce myself to you and welcome you to Bethel Baptist this morning. I know we haven't really met, but I know of you from my talks with Leonard. Please know that I am not your enemy, I'm just another woman who has the same wants and wishes as any other woman. Leonard and I never planned for this to happen, we were just friends and circumstances threw us together. I love him and want the best for him. I never meant to hurt you or anyone and I want you to know that I pray that you will find peace and that God will place someone in your life."

Reaching out to take Cleo's hand Rachel nodded her head and turned to walk away. She stopped after taking a few steps and turned to Cleopatra. "I hope you and Leonard will be happy. You are truly blessed to have those two adorable children. May God be with you."

*   *   *

Sunday dinner had been prepared by Della Handy to celebrate the announcement of Leonard and Cleopatra's engagement. Pat, Annette, Kathy and Poopie were in attendance as were Mr. and Mrs. Beavers. Everyone was enjoying themselves and the wonderful meal prepared by Mrs. Handy. Rev. Handy brought out a bottle of champagne and served each adult with a flute while giving the children a cup of white grape juice.

Bringing up her flute of champagne in the air, Annette made a loud whistle. "May I have everyone's attention please? I would like to make a toast to the happy couple and I wish them years and years of wedded bliss. Although in the beginning I had my doubts about Leonard, I know if he makes Cleopatra this happy he must be a good man. I would also like to apologize on behalf of the Golden Girls about the stains left on his Armani suit after he was busted upside the head with bowls of ice cream."

Pat, Kathy and Cleopatra howled with laughter. Rev. Handy, his wife and the Beavers had no clue as to what was going on.

When Leonard stood and told what happened, everyone laughed. "I must admit I deserved every drop of that ice cream," exclaimed Leonard. "I never dreamed someone as innocent looking as Cleopatra could connive with her friends and come up with such a plan. However, I can honestly say I have changed since then and God has answered my prayers. I only ask that all of you forgive me of my past indiscretions and know I will be the husband to Cleopatra that God demands I be. I love her more than I thought I could ever love any woman. She deserves to be happy and I will do everything in my power to keep her happy."

"Here, Here," shouted Mr. Beavers while Poopie sat and cried like the sissy he was. Pat, Annette and Kathy gathered around Poopie to tease their new friend.

*   *   *

Three months later as Cleopatra was getting Alexis ready for daycare so she could drop her off on her way to work someone rang her doorbell. Looking through the peephole, she could see a police car in the driveway and an older man in a suit and tie standing on her doorstep with someone standing behind him.

"May I help you," Cleo asked as she opened the door.

"Good morning, are you Cleopatra Beavers?"

Mercedes M. Alexander

"Yes, I am."

"My name is Lt. Marcus Martin of the Memphis police department and this is my partner, Drew Boyd. May we come in for a few minutes to discuss your husband's death?"

Beckoning the men to come in, Cleopatra led them to the living room and offered them a seat.

"Mrs. Beavers we have come to inform you this morning of the capture and arrest of the man we believe killed your husband. His name is Dennis Lairry and he was married to a woman who was having an affair with Michael Beavers. Tawanna Lairry was arrested a few weeks before your husband's death for fighting with another woman over him. She decided to take revenge out on Mr. Beavers and told her husband about the ongoing affair thinking he would just confront him and beat him up. She said she had no idea he would kill the man."

"Lt. Martin I am not surprised at all about the circumstances of my late husband's death. He gambled with his life for a long time by leading women on and playing with their affections. Most of the time men like him will eventually come to an end. However, I never thought Michael's end would result in such a horrid death. Thank you for being so kind and coming by this morning to inform me about the arrest. Now if you don't mind, I'm running behind time this morning and need to get my little girl to daycare."

"Yes Mrs. Beavers, sorry to have to come to you home with such bad news but, we were obligated to tell you in person before you read it in the newspaper or heard it on the news. We'll take our leave now and I hope you have a good day."

"Thank you officer, I hope your day goes well also."

Cleopatra's New Attitude

The two men walked to the door and got into their squad car. Cleo watched them until they backed out of the driveway. She was relieved to hear that Michael's murderer had been captured and decided to close the last chapter in the book of her life with Michael Beavers.

"Come on honey, it's time for mama to take you to school." Cleopatra picked up her daughter and headed out the door. Looking up at the sky she smiled and decided this was a good day. She put the child in her car seat, buckled her up and got in on the driver's side. As she backed out of her driveway, she made the instant decision to put her house up for sale. She would begin her new life in Leonard's home where there were no memories of Michael or her past life.

* * *

On April 2nd at precisely 3 p.m., Cleopatra Handy Beavers was walking down the aisle of Bethel Baptist Church on the arm of her father. She was radiant in a dress made of peach colored silk and Chantilly lace. The train of the dress was seven feet long and had Chantilly lace sewn around the edges. She was a vision of happiness and beauty. Walking right in front of her sprinkling flower pedals for her mother to walk on was little Alexis.

The church had been decorated by Poopie and his entourage of happy go lucky buddies. It was one of the most beautiful scenes anyone had seen for a wedding. There were peach and white roses everywhere and two towers of cascading water on each end of the pulpit. Each pew was decorated elaborately with peach Chantilly laced bows. There was netting hanging from the ceiling of the grand church with peach and white flower petals. The walls in the church sparkled with thousands of little twinkling lights and behind the pulpit and the waterfalls was a backdrop that looked as if someone had placed a garden in the sanctuary. The backdrop had little twinkling lights in the sky. To give all of this the grand effect, the lights in the church were turned completely off. The only light in the church came from the 100 candles on each side of the waterfalls and the twinkling lights.

The people gasped in awe as the lights were dimmed and the bride started her walk down the aisle.

Standing at the front of the beautifully decorated church was Leonard with Matthew at his side as the ring bearer. Pat, Annette and Kathy were Cleo's attendants. They were wearing long strapless dresses in a darker shade of peach. Leonard dressed in a white tuxedo with a peach colored shirt and white bow tie had three of his fraternity brothers dressed in white tuxedos and white shirts with peach colored bow ties as his groomsmen.

As Leonard and Cleopatra's eyes met, both of them smiled. Today was the beginning of their lives together and there were 300 people in the church to witness their vows. People smiled and nodded their heads as they watch Cleopatra walk down the aisle.

The minister read from the book of Ephesians and announced to everyone that Leonard and Cleopatra had written their own vows. When Leonard looked into his bride's eyes to say his vows, he brought her hands to his lips.

"As I stand here today before God and man, I declare my devotion to you Cleopatra. I never knew what happiness was until you became a part of my life. I love you and pray daily for you. I think of you when I wake up each morning, all through the day and when I close my eyes at night. I dream of you while I sleep and when I awake each morning, I start the

Cleopatra's New Attitude

process of thinking of you all over again. You have become my very being, my soul mate, my friend, my love. I will be faithful, honest and devoted to you. I vow to take you as my beloved wife, the mother of our children and I will cherish you all the days of my life."

Sliding the wedding band on Cleopatra's finger, Leonard felt a tear slide down his face. Cleopatra saw it too, reached up, and wiped it away with her fingers. She then looked up at Leonard and held his hand to repeat her vows to him.

"I have been blessed by God to find real happiness and fulfillment as a woman. Leonard, you have been my guardian angel and I know you were sent to me by God. I thank you for your patience, love and kindness. As I stand here today before this congregation, I pledge my love to you and promise to be a virtuous woman, a devoted wife and a good mother to our children. I promised to love, honor and obey you. Today I become bone of your bone and flesh of your flesh. Where you go I will follow. For all the days of my life I will love and cherish you."

Sliding a wedding ring on Leonard's hand, Cleopatra smiled contently and looked down at her children.

The couple was then instructed to kneel as the minister prayed for their marriage and the two children they had been charged by God to raise. When Cleo and Leonard kneeled, little Alexis made her way to kneel between the two of them with Matthew following her lead. There was a sigh of happiness from everyone in the church.

After the prayer the minister asked the couple to stand, he then said, "I now pronounce you man and wife, what God has put together let no man put asunder. You may now kiss your bride."

Mercedes M. Alexander

As Leonard pulled Cleopatra toward him, he whispered to her "I love you Mrs. Wilkins."

"I love you too honey," was her response just before he placed his lips gently on his wife's, the woman he would now love and cherish forever.

CPSIA information can be obtained at www.ICGtesting.com
Printed in the USA
LVOW092058080612

285269LV00002B/6/P